THE FOURTH LETTY CAMPBELL MYSTERY

ALMA FRITCHLEY
chicken shack

First published by The Women's Press Ltd, 2000
A member of the Namara Group
34 Great Sutton Street, London EC1V OLQ
www.the-womens-press.com

British Library Cataloguing-in-Publication Data.
A catalogue record for this book is available from the British Library.

ISBN 0 7043 4686 9

Typeset in Plantin 11/12pt by FiSH Books, London
Printed and bound in Great Britain by Cox & Wyman, Reading, Berkshire

This book is dedicated to Eileen.
The bravest woman I know.

Acknowledgements

Thanks to all my friends and colleagues at Manchester
Tax Office for their selfless support!
Special mention goes to Carole, Julie, Christine, Bill,
Marian, Diane and Susan, not forgetting Sarah Jayne
and the rest of the gang for doling out ideas on demand.
I am particularly grateful for the literary advice offered
by Maria Smith and Fran Bell.
I especially appreciate the help of techies Damian and
Mark for averting disaster at forty thousand words.
And thanks to all at The Women's Press, in particular
Kirsty Dunseath for being the best editor on
the planet (any planet).
Love, above all, to Eileen for being there.
And cheers to Dad and Ann for all those trips to the library!

Chapter 1

Julia Rossi, my best friend and one-time lover, had finally lost the plot.

'How much land do you own, exactly?' she asked, giving me a long sideways glance from under her floppy fringe. Those piercing grey eyes, inherited from her Italian parents, tried and failed to hide the obvious monetary interest.

I sighed. As if she didn't know. She knew my finances, my love life (or lack of it) and every other aspect of my existence as well as I did.

Better, sometimes, which was annoying.

I gazed across the land in question. Even the bright spring sunlight of this May Bank Holiday didn't illuminate one end of my property to the other. My current acreage covered more than the eye could see. Julia reckoned that at the rate I was inheriting land – firstly my chicken farm left to me by my Aunt Cynthia whose questionable past had made my independence possible, and now the spread next door bequeathed to me by Cynthia's wartime lover – I would end up owning half of Yorkshire.

I didn't want to own half of Yorkshire. I didn't know

what to do with the land I'd already *got*.

My neighbours had been full of suggestions, though.

'A cinema would be nice,' chirped my old friend Mrs Buckham, owner of Calderton's corner. 'You could have theme nights.'

'Theme nights?'

'Or eras,' the elderly woman had proposed.

'Eras?'

'Victorian, Edwardian . . .'

'Did they have cinema in those days?' I asked, wide-eyed.

'Silent, then. Thirties gangster films. War films, cowboy films, martial arts films. Gay films.' She smiled at me, thinking that would clinch it.

'I wouldn't get planning permission,' I pointed out.

'You don't need it.' She sniffed. 'I know the farm-house has been knocked down, but you could convert the old barn. It's big enough. Who'd ever know?'

I didn't point out that knowing Calderton's bush telegraph the whole world would get wind of it by teatime.

As a stopgap I'd rented part of the property to Stan, a neighbouring farmer. As Julia and I surveyed the fields, several dozen sheep and their new offspring, just past the cute lamb stage, nibbled idly at the grass. Lamb chops to some, a new winter coat to others, money in the bank to me. God, I was getting more farmer-like with each passing day.

I turned to Julia. 'Shouldn't you be at work?'

Reluctantly, she checked her watch. 'Eight o'clock. Another half-hour yet and knowing my luck my buyer is bound to be late – they're never on time. I *hate* working on bank holidays,' she moaned, scraping mud from the soles of her highly polished Chelsea boots. She left a small mound of muck and grass on the bottom rung of the fencing on which we were leaning. 'I think you should consider my suggestion, though.'

'Julia,' I groaned. 'Mrs Buckham's cinema idea's got more going for it. A health farm? In Calderton? Who'd come? . . . No, who in their *right mind* would come?' I corrected. She grinned and a gold-capped tooth glinted in the sunlight.

Though forty-odd, Julia acted (and admitted she felt) as though she only just hit thirty. I suspected HRT, though she adamantly denied it. 'You'll know when I'm menopausal,' she'd threatened. I'd known Julia for more than ten years and had lived through every disaster and every trauma, whether work, woman or family related, she'd ever suffered. Life, for her, was sweet at the moment, hence the heavy involvement in my affairs. She'd been with her current lover, Sita Joshi, our local MP, for a couple of years and her job as part-owner and saleswoman at the local garage kept her in cars, and the bank in business. The only continuing cross she had to bear was her work colleague AnnaMaria, my previous lover's niece.

Honestly, it's not as complicated as it sounds . . .

Julia looked at her watch again and continued in the same persuasive tones. 'Actually, I could probably supply you with a list of who would come. It would be more popular than you think.'

That hung in the air for a moment or two.

'Oh, I don't know, Julia,' I sighed, trying to envision the sort of exclusive club she thought would be successful. 'It's a million miles away from farming after all. Imagine what the villagers would say about it. And the council would certainly kick up a stink. God, the uproar.'

'As long as it's used for something, I can't see the

3

problem,' she retorted, and then seeing my face, laughed. 'All right, all right, I get the message.' She went quiet for a moment but the silence was obviously killing her. I should have known she couldn't let it rest. 'The thing is,' she went on, all wide-eyed and innocent.

'The thing is?'

She looked into the distance and weighed her words carefully. 'Well, how much interest has your advert stirred, hmm?'

I followed her gaze. 'Not much,' I admitted.

'One,' Julia said firmly. 'You've had one bite, Letty.'

My attempts to sell, lease or otherwise get rid of this excess of land had failed despite repeat adverts in farming magazines and the local press. In all honesty, the property didn't have much going for it. With the recent furore surrounding genetically modified foods and farming being in such a slump, the spectacular indifference shown to George's place had come as no great surprise. The farmhouse was long gone, its infrastructure ruined by extensive flooding, years of neglect, a rotten roof and El Niño-type storms the previous year. The barn hadn't been in quite the same sorry state and an insurance payout had ensured its survival (and reinvention as extremely generous living quarters) for at least another hundred years. Even so, I'd been disappointed by the non-response to the adverts. I sighed again: perhaps I'd be stuck with it for ever.

'The problem,' I said, 'is that this one bite you are so fond of reminding me about was from an acquaintance of yours and frankly, Julia, that worries me.'

'You have no faith,' she insisted, hiding a smile.

'And is there any wonder! You and your friends have dropped me in the shit often enough in the past. Or have you forgotten?'

4

Julia squirmed, though it didn't take her long to get over it.

'This woman has contacts you wouldn't dream about. Good contacts. *Loaded* contacts,' she added with some force.

'You've been trying to convince me for, how long now? I lease or sell the land, your *contact* organises everything from there.' There was an odd feeling of déjà vu about this conversation, I'd been down a similar route before; cajoled too easily by Julia's soft-soaping.

'Exactly!' Julia chimed in. 'A simple solution, and a temporary one, if you want it to be.' She draped an arm around my shoulders and gave me a hug. 'It'll give you something else to think about,' she whispered in my ear. 'You know Anne's moving to London soon, you can't fret about her for ever.'

Now that stung. Anne, AnnaMaria's aunt, had been my partner for six years until she'd found herself a younger, richer and more experienced model. Christ, an-everything-I-wasn't model. For months I'd felt like an old racehorse put out to pasture.

'That's not fair, Julia,' I protested. But it was, and she was right. She squeezed my shoulder again. 'Look,' I conceded. 'I'll talk to AnnaMaria about it. She might not want that kind of place on her doorstep.' AnnaMaria had lived in my attic with her young son since his birth more than three years ago. 'You know how she gets with those snotty types you knock about with. And she's been on the receiving end of some of your hare-brained schemes too. They haven't always been pleasant experiences.' I made another futile attempt to remind her of her dodgy past.

Julia's grin broadened and she kissed my cheek. 'Letty,' she said. 'You're a wonderful woman. I never

5

believe anything they say about you.'

'Who – ?' I began and then realised she was joking. 'Go to work, go to work. Sell some cars for God's sake. Do what you're good at,' I said and shooed her away.

Chapter 2

'You're going to do it, aren't you?' AnnaMaria declared over breakfast half an hour later.

I looked across the table in surprise. A spoonful of cornflakes was halfway to her lips and a bruised banana was clutched in her other hand. Her son, Liam, was meticulously peeling every scrap of shell from a boiled egg. It looked as though it would take him hours.

'Would you mind?' I asked her. She took a chunk of the banana and swallowed without bothering to chew.

'Not if it will stop you moping,' she said. I gazed at her slim, urchin features and sighed. She'd just hate it if she knew she'd echoed Julia's sentiments.

'You've got to let it go, you know. Or get hold of it and get mad. Whichever.' She swallowed the rest of the fruit and shovelled cornflakes into her mouth.

'I did get mad,' I pointed out. I remembered, with a great deal of discomfort, a screaming match I'd had with her aunt. The memory still gave me a headache.

'You're reminiscing again,' AnnaMaria interrupted. 'Look, if you want a holiday camp next door –'

'Health farm.'

'– then just do it. Who cares? I don't. You shouldn't.

Liam certainly doesn't.'

My eyes drifted to the little boy. A whole egg displaced his right cheek.

'Chew it,' AnnaMaria commanded. Liam looked at his mum and smiled. Despite the egg, his face mirrored hers – fair hair and hazel eyes. He began to chew and crumbly egg white cascaded on to the pine table.

'You are so messy,' AnnaMaria complained half-heartedly. She only had herself to blame, she led by example in the table manners department.

'It doesn't bother you then? That one of Julia's "associates" is involved.'

'Huh, I can handle Julia,' she said emphatically, 'and her *associates.*'

'So, thumbs up or down then?' I pressed her to take the decision from me.

'Up, definitely. It might keep Julia away from the garage for a bit as well.' She grinned and began to scrape crumbs from the table into her hand, humming as she did so. Already she saw herself running the garage as she'd like with only limited interference from her supposed ally in the motoring world. She took the crumbs to the back door and slung them at the chickens. World War Three began and ended in seconds.

I thought about Julia's idea and AnnaMaria's enthusiasm and suddenly, for no obvious reason, I felt relieved. Already the prospect was taking my mind off . . . what, precisely?

Anne's absence, for a start. And loneliness too. Despite a house full of people I felt a sense of isolation I'd not experienced for years. And I was bored. Busy, but bored. I shared my life mostly with chickens, and I didn't want to share my intellect with them as well.

I needed stimulation, and in more ways than one.

Pondering this, I cleared the breakfast pots as AnnaMaria whisked Liam off to his great-aunt's for a few days. As difficult as it was for me, AnnaMaria wanted to keep her relationship with Anne on as normal a level as possible. My ex had only moved to the next village and despite her new lover, her life hadn't really changed much at all.

Fortunately our paths rarely crossed.

'Oh fuck this,' I said to myself and, leaving the rest of the pots, I stomped outside. The chickens screamed in panic as though Ozzy Osbourne had just dropped in. Stupid creatures. As a vegetarian I was the least likely person to lop their heads off. I was the only chicken farmer I knew that let their livestock die of old age. If I wasn't careful the farm would end up more like a bird sanctuary than a going concern. Thank God Aunt Cynthia had left me enough money to be so indulgent.

I watched as the chickens strutted about the place, clucking demonically. For sanity's sake I needed to do something physical.

Chapter 3

I can do that, I thought as I gazed at the broken guttering waving gently in the breeze. The plastic squeaked against the downspout; a good shower would bring it crashing to earth.

Ten years ago I would have been on the phone to a builder; even five years ago my attempts at DIY would have been botched at best. Dad had drummed it into me: 'Stick with what you know.' Once I'd only have known how to shuffle papers around an office but nowadays I'd have a crack at most things.

The huge barn out back housed everything a farmer could need: a fully equipped slaughterhouse (my aunt hadn't had the same qualms as me), tools and provisions, foodstuffs and hardware. Some of the relics would surely be worth something. It reminded me of an old pub I'd read about that hadn't been touched since 1963. *Antique Roadshow* presenters would have been drooling.

My own particularly useful bits and pieces were at the back of the barn, neatly stacked on shelves or stored in simple wooden cupboards. I retrieved a green Army stores utility belt, an item that Julia had given me.

'It was Jackie's, you remember Jackie,' she'd explained when presenting it. 'She wanted it for a fetish party, but her girlfriend thought it was a bit eighties.'

I'd stared at her, but the look she'd given me was ingenuous. Years spent on a farm had forced fetish out of my vocabulary, while Julia could bandy it about without even a smirk.

The garment had come in useful though. It held a hammer, ultra-light cordless drill, nails and bits of piping, and I could wear it without dislocating any of my joints.

I slipped it around my waist and its familiar weight nestled against my hips. I tried to imagine it around a fetishist's body but somehow couldn't summon up the picture. Perhaps it had never hung from Jackie's waist after all and was destined for more exotic territory. I really needed to get out more...

I took the ladder from the side of the barn and wedged it just below my bedroom window. Over the last few years I'd just about managed to conquer my fear of heights and, zipping up the ladder, I set to work on the guttering.

I'd just sunk the last screw into the wooden support when the frantic fluttering of wings announced a visitor.

'Yo, Letty.' Who did I know from a Spike Lee film? A tentative glance over my shoulder, and the familiar if somewhat unexpected face of Emma Auckland, the local bobby, stared back at me.

In these parts the arrival of the police doesn't necessarily mean trouble. I hoped Emma would bear that in mind.

'Two minutes, Emma,' I promised, fiddling with roofing nails.

'No rush,' she stated. Emma's conservative use of

11

language was legendary. Why use a whole sentence when two words would do? I heard her clatter up the porch steps and recognised the creak of the rocking chair as she made herself comfortable. From my vantage point I could see Calderton's police van parked on the far reaches of my drive. A familiar figure was perched on the front seat; Mrs Buckham, hair a steely grey halo around her pale face. Her hands clutched an enormous handbag with a vice-like grip. Knowing my old friend's mistrust of the police (and her vivid imagination), she probably thought they'd slip something incriminating into it if she took her eyes off it for one second.

I joined Emma on the porch.

'Tea?' I asked.

'Milk, one sugar,' she informed me.

'Will she want one?' I asked, vaguely indicating the whereabouts of my neighbour.

'Only if you make it.'

Mrs Buckham wouldn't put a spot of poisoning past the guardians of the law either. Something significant must have happened to compel her to climb into a van with a member of Calderton's police force.

Emma followed me into the kitchen.

I noticed, with a sort of half-interest, that she had finally succumbed to wearing the new-style uniform. Calderton's small troop had held out far longer than their big city neighbours but finally the tall hats and heavy coats had been replaced by bomber jackets and LAPD-style pants and accessories. If the word accessory can be used to describe gas canisters and Ninja nightsticks.

Mind you, Emma still wore the same stupid hat WPCs had been wearing for years. Same stupid check cravat, too. She took the stupid hat off as I handed her the tea.

'Shall I take this one out –?'

'Don't bother,' Emma interrupted. 'She'll come in shortly.'

I left Mrs Buckham's brew on the table.

'What's up then?'

Emma 'asbestos mouth' Auckland downed her tea in two quick swallows and wiped her lips indelicately on the back of her hand.

'Gas leak,' she said. 'Big one.'

'Where?' I asked, chopping my words to suit the occasion.

'Corner shop. Out of bounds.'

'Gas board?'

'Not them. But it's being fixed.'

'How long?'

'A week.'

We'd be into sign language at this rate.

'And she wants to stay here?' I ventured.

Emma nodded.

'She could have rung,' I said, realising that the unofficial open-door policy I seemed to run for the temporarily homeless was about to be instigated again. (You name a friend, a relative or a vague aquaintance and at some time or other, they'd lodged at my farm).

Emma shrugged and got up. Retrieving her hat she ventured beyond silence and monosyllables. 'It's okay, isn't it? I'll get her bags.' I didn't seem to have much choice.

'A week, you say,' I said, groping for some control. Though Mrs Buckham and I had been friends for years, and had shared many experiences, we'd never actually stayed under the same roof for any length of time.

'Just say if you mind,' she replied brusquely.

'What about her sister?' Even as I said it, I knew there was no chance.

'Only one bedroom. And it's supported housing.'

'And Janice?' I asked desperately. Mrs Buckham's niece, a reporter for the local paper, *the Calderton Echo*, had recently got married. And while even I knew Janice and her spouse earned enough for a decent mortgage, it seemed curious that they'd settled on a one-bedroomed flat. Or maybe not so curious after all . . .

I caught a slight shake of Emma's head and a mumbled 'What am I? A social worker?'

I sighed an agreement and followed her out of the house.

Chapter 4

'Drives like a maniac and hardly said a word,' Mrs
Buckham complained as she took a seat on the porch. 'I
told her I didn't need a lift, but she reckoned she was
heading this way. Ha! Thinks I'm past it. I could give her
a run for her money. Doesn't even trust me to get a taxi.
Patronising, if you ask me. And I told her you wouldn't
mind. It's only for a few days. Well, according to the Gas
people, but what they say and what they do aren't always
the same.' She took a breath before going on. 'I've
arranged for a refit too, might as well while the place is
shut.' She looked at me closely, gauging my reaction.
'You don't mind, do you?'

'No,' I said with as much conviction as I could
muster. 'I'll show you the spare room.'

'Oh, it'll keep.' The elderly woman waved my
suggestion away, the vague shooing motion a sign of
relief. 'I've stayed over before. It's not like I don't know
where it is.'

We sat in silence as a brisk but warm May wind
whipped feathers and farm dust around our feet. I tried
to ignore inbuilt warning signals.

'Is there anything you need from the shop? Clothes?

Videos?' I asked, a note of despair creeping into my voice.

'Ooh no, I've got everything I need for the moment. All my other stuff is being put into storage as we speak. It'll be locked up tight until I go back.' She shuffled for a more comfortable position on the rocking chair and her pink puffa jacket hissed as air escaped from between the fibres. Over the last few months Mrs Buckham had abandoned the floral, old lady's frocks she'd always worn. A catalogue delivered by mistake from a factory seconds shop had revolutionised her wardrobe. Polyester had been exchanged for cotton mixes and materials I couldn't even put a name to. Her jacket, the familiar Kappa design running up both sleeves, clashed wonderfully with neon-bright, blue lycra leggings. At least she'd never get run over.

'Those pipes hadn't been looked at in years,' Mrs Buckham went on. 'Rotten they were, the gas man said. Should have been replaced ages ago. I was lucky I suppose.'

'Lucky! You could have been blown to bits.'

'No, not about that. The leaking pipes were just that side of council property. Another foot nearer and it would have cost me a fortune.'

I stifled a laugh as this particular silver lining attached itself to Mrs Buckham's cloud.

'I'll help around the house of course. Can't stand being idle. First time I've not been able to open that shop since . . .' She thought for a moment and shuffled again. Her coat made slightly vulgar noises. 'Since the floorboards were replaced, ages back.' She paused. 'I could look after Liam, save AnnaMaria the bother of childminders.'

This had, in fact, been a problem of late. AnnaMaria's

long-standing and, some would say, long-suffering ex-boyfriend, Andy, still had a hand in Liam's upbringing and helped out when she needed a break. What made this all the more surprising was the fact that Liam wasn't actually Andy's son. The identity of the little boy's father was still a mystery to all but AnnaMaria.

In her various relationships over the years AnnaMaria had chosen, if I can put this delicately, rather unusual partners sometimes. The fling she'd had with a woman when she was in her teens had ended in, well, tears is too limp a description. A long-distance, if short-lived, affair with a rabbi from Tel Aviv had put the cat among the chickens as far as Calderton Village was concerned. But for the moment she was alone. Alone and loving it.

'She would like that,' I reassured my old friend. Mrs Buckham beamed.

Idly she kicked her rather fashionable trainers across the porch and waggled her toes. 'That's better,' she muttered. 'I think I'm getting a corn,' and she hoisted her left leg on to her right knee. 'I wonder if it's a verruca.'

We both peered at the source of her pain. 'Hard skin,' I informed her with relief. She prodded it for a few seconds then looked at me and said airily, 'Anne was in the other day. She bought some of your eggs. She'll miss them when she moves.'

Secretly I hoped they'd choke her but I didn't voice my thoughts. There was a good chance that such an uncharitable suggestion would get back to my ex-partner. I was down, but not quite out.

Chapter 5

'It'll be your mother,' Mrs Buckham insisted as she helped me give the house a quick tidy. 'It's ages since she called round.'

But whoever was on their way up my drive, it wasn't my mum. 'She's in Scotland,' I explained wearily. 'With the Colonel.' Sylvia Buckham could be such hard work.

Now retired, officially at least, my mother, Margaret Campbell, had found a new lease of life. If travel was a drug, then she was a junkie. Her job as PA to Colonel Thompson, old-fashioned solicitor in equally old-fashioned premises, had come to an end, though their relationship hadn't stopped there. And I use the term loosely. I had my own suspicions as far as her friendship with her boss went. Mum had been a widow for years, and somehow I felt that we'd be hearing wedding bells soon. Knowing my mother, she'd probably tell me after the event, or the invite would come from some tiny island in the Caribbean.

But I had a good idea who this suprise guest might be. AnnaMaria had rung me from the garage warning me of an imminent arrival. 'Some old bag Julia knows,' my tenant had growled over the phone. 'Julia says she's going to make you an offer you can't refuse.'

I felt like fleeing the country.

'Nobody I know,' Mrs Buckham said, staring out of the kitchen window.

I peered over her shoulder. 'Nope,' I agreed. 'Looks like a new face to me.'

In fact, it was a new face in one of Julia's newer cars. I knew the big Renault had been on the forecourt for only a short while.

Julia and AnnaMaria pulled in behind her. My ex still drove a red MGF and AnnaMaria drove any old thing that was available – on this occasion an Astra, belching smoke. She'd got rid of her Mondeo when the insurance skyrocketed. 'If I'm going to pay those sort of premiums, I may as well save up for something worth having,' she'd said to me one day. Her latest fancy – not everybody's idea of 'something worth having' – was a Suzuki Vitara, and I knew exactly which one she wanted. A five-year-old model, in white, gathered dust at the back of Rossi and Marple Motors. 'It's waiting for parts,' AnnaMaria had explained, going into technical speak to flummox her associate, who had enough mechanical knowledge to pull the wool over the eyes of less informed customers, but not enough to contradict AnnaMaria's insistence on a new camshaft and rotary arm. She could have said *rotisserie* and Julia would have been none the wiser.

And waiting for parts? I don't think so. Waiting for AnnaMaria's bank balance to be sufficiently swollen to buy it more like. I knew what she was up to. Every time Julia made threatening sounds such as, 'Get it on the forecourt, now,' the Japanese vehicle would develop some strange new fault. One week it would squeal, another week it would rattle and sometimes it just wouldn't do anything at all.

The three women headed for my house and Mrs Buckham busied herself with tea-making duties.

Julia had taken to wearing skirts of late; she'd heeded my comment that I thought she had fantastic legs, and Sita couldn't keep her hands off her the more flesh she exposed. The charcoal grey pin-striped Versace number she wore showed off her terrific full-bodied figure. Youthful and willowy in contrast, AnnaMaria trudged, scowling, through the door.

Julia flung her briefcase triumphantly on the kitchen table.

'Letty, I'd like you to meet Amy.'

'Amy' peered round AnnaMaria's tense shoulder and smiled.

Now I've read lots of American novels and when Stephen King or Patricia Cornwell described someone as 'preppy' I was never quite sure what they meant. Until I clapped eyes on Amy. She looked so neat and clean you could have eaten your dinner off her. Her fair hair was short, combed and untroubled by the breezy May weather. Her clothes were as neat as her hair.

I'll work my way up from the feet. Navy blue sandals. Size f▓▓▓▓▓▓▓▓▓▓▓▓▓▓▓▓▓▓ ... cool blue cotton. John Lewis? Certainly their style. Knitted lemon cotton cardigan, a broad blue band stretching across the middle to add to that college look. Hand made? Probably by Agnès b. or Nicole Farhi. (I know these things – Julia is my best friend, remember?) Calf skin, satchel-type shoulder bag. Expensive? What do you think?

She was wholesome and healthy, fresh faced and fanciable, pretty in a sanitary-towel-ad sort of way. I would never, ever have guessed she was a mate of Julia's. Julia didn't have this type of friend. Usually they were scary business types, hung up on money, cars, sex and busy grappling for purchase on that greasy pole. I was the one exception to the rule.

Amy smiled at me and scanned my face with her clear blue eyes. When she opened her mouth I half expected an American accent. What I got was, well, I don't really know. I could normally tell a Lancashire accent from a Yorkshire one, and Cheshire from Mancunian was dead easy but the strange hybrid that tripped off Amy's tongue was completely new to me.

'Hello, Letty. It's good to meet you,' she said in a quiet voice. I smiled and we shook hands. Her skin was smooth and well scrubbed and her nails, apart from an overly long thumbnail, were clipped and clean.

I looked at Julia and waited for an explanation.

Naturally she obliged. 'Amy has made some enquiries about next door's farm.'

'Oh?'

'I'd like to buy it, if we can agree to a price,' Amy said. 'And the sooner the better.'

'Not cheap, the land round here, you know,' Mrs Buckham butted in, slamming the tea on the table. 'Ripe for development they say. Farming's going to be a thing of the past, you mark my words,' she insisted, though she didn't suggest what the alternative to farming might be.

Amy looked bemused. 'Are you from the estate agent's?' she asked politely.

AnnaMaria, thawing slightly, suppressed a giggle.

'Best friend and neighbour. I only have Letty's interests at heart,' Mrs Buckham replied frostily.

'I'll let you have the agent's address, if you haven't already got it,' I interrupted, waving Amy into a chair. 'And my solicitor's. Finances can be discussed through her. Make an offer and I'll let you know.'

This was all a bit too quick for me. Calderton didn't usually work this way. Even haggling at a market stall took ages. Tea was served in silence by an offended Mrs Buckham. The silence stretched to engulf us all. I felt something more was expected of me, though I didn't know what.

'I think Julia explained about the health farm,' Amy began. She smiled a toothy smile. 'Though health farm is a bit of an outdated term nowadays, and rather inaccurate too. My client...'

'Client? What client?' Mrs Buckham interrupted, mid pour.

'Oh, I'm sorry. Hasn't it been made clear? I'm not interested in the property myself. I'm an agent for a client who desperately requires premises. My firm has represented the organisation all over the States.'

Perhaps that's where her 'look' came from.

She continued. 'This is their first foray into Britain. Apparently, they fell in love with this area when they first visited a few years ago. They stayed at the farm next door in fact, when it was a bed and breakfast establishment.'

'More fool them,' Mrs Buckham sniffed.

Old George had owned it then, before eventually, in a roundabout way, it had come to me. Americans, perhaps not knowing any better, had thought the old farm 'enchanting'. About as enchanting as the council dump after a three-month bin strike. Amy glanced at the faces around the table as she took a cup of tea on offer.

'Why out here?' I asked. Julia took up the story, missing my point.

'From what Amy has said, it's needed as a kind of retreat. A holistic retreat. You know, escape from life's stresses and strains.'

It was the sort of claptrap Julia normally came out with. AnnaMaria sighed, loudly.

'And they want to buy the farm? It'll be a permanent set-up then?' I asked.

'Assuming the finances are agreeable, yes. Leasing is an option too. I understand you've leased your land before,' Amy said smoothly. I had, and wondered how Amy knew this snippet. 'Of course,' she went on, 'this sort of venture isn't cheap and it has to be viable in a business sense. But I think you'll find my clients have the necessary resources.' She paused and fiddled with her cup. 'I wanted to meet you to pave the way really, Letty. My clients didn't want you to have any major problems with the ethics of it all.'

Had she mistaken me for the Dalai Lama? Ethics? As long as the farm wasn't being used to film porn (giving *Animal Farm* a whole new meaning), or house new Tory Party headquarters, then the highest bidder could take it off my hands with my blessing.

'If people want to beat a retreat, then it's fine by me,' I attempted a joke with a shrug. 'There isn't much leeway as far as the price is concerned,' I cautioned her. 'But as I said, you can thrash it out with the solicitor.'

Amy smiled. 'I'll let Chris know.' We looked at her blankly. 'The main organiser of the group.'

'Who are they?' I asked suspiciously. 'Are they a spiritual . . . organisation?' I nearly choked on the word.

'Well, not strictly speaking, though I think there may be a trace of it running through their enterprise. We have to respect client confidentiality so I wouldn't really like to comment. My employer wanted me to place them in suitable accommodation in England. They call themselves CFC, the letters are Chris's initials, though the financial backing comes via the family. The father, to be specific. It's a paternal thing,' she said and smiled weakly. I felt that the moment's pause that followed hinted at some hidden meaning. But if there was enlightenment to be had, it eluded me.

'But the interests of *my* firm are purely financial,' Amy continued eventually. 'Anyway, I'll have to be going. Here's my card should you need to get in touch, and I've got some leaflets here.' She rummaged in her bag. 'They may be of benefit if you feel you need to know more about my client.' She put a leatherette folder on the table, CFC embossed in gold in one corner. Unable to resist, Mrs Buckham fingered it curiously. 'Can I trouble you for your solicitor's address, if you've got it handy?'

It was my turn to do a bit of rummaging, and I produced the required information from a drawer by the sink.

Amy got up, hoisting her bag on to her shoulder. 'I need to take some measurements and photos if that's all right. It seems pointless to go to the estate agent's just to come back again.' She looked at me hopefully.

'Fine,' I said, and hunted through the same kitchen drawer for the keys. 'The barn's been completely renovated, not the old shack it used to be,' I explained, leading Amy to the door. 'It's stone built. The plumbing and the electrics are all new. It's a huge place. Three floors and extra farm buildings at the back –'

'It's all right, Letty,' Amy interrupted, 'I can manage.' She moved away from me, one slender hand straightening invisible creases on her trousers.

AnnaMaria snorted unspoken disapproval and slammed out of the kitchen. Amy, with a curious backward glance, edged over the doorstep.

Mrs Buckham scrambled to the table and the pamphlet before I'd even had a chance to close the door.

'Sweet, isn't she?' Julia commented the minute Amy was out of earshot.

Sweet wasn't the word I would have chosen. 'She was okay, a bit mysterious though.'

'In what way?'

'Well, for a start, "A paternal thing." What the hell did that mean?'

'Oh, Letty, don't go reading into things. Daddy dishes out the money. Offspring does the hard work. It probably causes some bad feeling, you know how people are when it comes to money. Not everyone can be like me. Unquestioningly accepting funds from their parents,' Julia said, her eyes twinkling.

I laughed at the unaccustomed honesty. 'Well, she wasn't your usual type,' I snorted.

'Type of what?' Julia feigned indignance.

'Well, she didn't whip out a laptop or a cheque book to start with. And she didn't treat me like an oink either.'

'My friends don't treat you like that!' The indignation was real now. 'Sita loves you to bits.'

'There are rules and then there are exceptions,' I pointed out. After all, I was one of them.

Mrs Buckham rattled the papers she'd immersed herself in.

'She was efficient.' I relented.

Julia forgave me my comments and bent to look in the fridge. "She's new to the firm apparently, so she's bound to be. You wouldn't think people would find it so hard to find suitable premises, would you? Useless bastards some of her clients. Couldn't find the loo without a map.'

'How do you know her then?' I asked, straining for a peep over Mrs Buckham's shoulder.

'Well, to be honest I don't really know *her*,' Julia continued, from the depths of the fridge. 'But Sita's dealt with her firm before. They found her flat for her. You know how busy she is, never finds the time for anything. Always dashing to London for her meetings and whatnot. They organised her furnishings too. Sita would be sleeping on the floor if it wasn't for Amy's company,' she went on blithely, totally unaware that she'd managed to insult her partner.

Julia had located my stash of olives and promptly popped one into her mouth. 'Got any hummus? I'm starving.'

'Behind the eggs, there's bread on the side,' I informed her absently.

'I always get like this when I'm mid-cycle,' she muttered. 'Water retention, pain, blood, perpetual hunger. Who'd be a woman?'

'Julia, do you mind?' I said.

A tut from Mrs Buckham drew me back to the kitchen table.

'How can people believe all this rubbish?' she asked pointedly. 'What happened to common sense? Eh? Letty, just listen to this.' She cleared her throat before pretending to quote from one of the glossy pamphlets. "For a thousand pounds a week you can eat lettuce and run around starkers to your heart's content..."'

Julia guffawed and an olive stone bounced across the floor. 'It doesn't say that!'

'It might as well,' Mrs Buckham said, slapping the booklet against the tabletop. 'A retreat, my eye. A week in Blackpool would do them more good. A damn sight cheaper too.'

I prised the booklet from her hand. 'CFC. An introduction...' it read.

We at CFC believe true happiness, health and vitality

can be achieved despite the strains of everyday life. A regime of healthy food, quiet and retrospective contemplation, exercises or the unintrusive expert surgery that is to be made available at our sister clinic in Manchester; all are designed to suit your personal needs.

Unintrusive surgery? Face lifts, I presumed. Colonic irrigation? Liposuction, perhaps? My mind went into overdrive. And sister clinic? What precisely, was that?

I read on.

We offer you more than just an escape. We offer you the chance to cleanse body and soul, to discover a NEW YOU.

If you would like to know more, please contact the toll-free number below.

'Toll-free number?' Julia mumbled. 'Isn't that an Americanism?'

The whole thing was cheesy as far as I was concerned. we shuffled through the other papers. Available services and therapies were listed. From mud-laden beauty treatments to wind-surfing and hot spas. Guests could enrol in courses in Feng Shui (what else); participate in the dance/self defence art of Brazilian Copeira, or take a chance on a curiosity entitled 'stunt aerobics'. The virtues of all these 'treatments' were espoused as though they were a cure all for the problems of the world.

'Stunt aerobics sounds a bit scary, but the rest looks fairly harmless,' Julia decided. 'Might spend a couple of days there myself, once they're up and running. Windsurfing sounds like my kind of thing.'

'Where?' I asked.

'Where what?'

'Where would you wind surf in Calderton?'

Julia looked puzzled. 'The reservoir?'

I sighed. 'Julia, when was the last time you did any exercise? I mean real exercise, not just running from the car to the offy before it shuts.'

She looked offended. 'I did that kick-boxing course.'

Mrs Buckham piped up. 'That must be five years ago.'

Julia turned her back. 'I was quite good at that. Never missed a lesson.'

'It was only a six-week course,' I reminded her.

'Anyway,' Julia said, trying to rescue the moment. 'What are you saying? That I'm getting past it? Or fat?' She turned sideways on and patted her stomach, which, despite a lack of physical activity, was as flat as ever. 'My weight hasn't fluctuated more than half a stone since –'

'Julia, keep your vest on,' Mrs Buckham said. 'Nobody's saying that. It's just that windsurfing can be a bit, you know. Exhausting.'

I tried to read Sylvia Buckham's expression. What was she getting at?

'I know something much better than getting wet in the reservoir,' she hinted.

We waited.

'Keeps you fit too.' The silence lengthened.

'It's free.'

'What?' we asked together.

Please don't say sex, I begged soundlessly.

'Sex!' she shrilled.

Julia turned to me and mouthed, 'How do you put up with her?'

I shrugged. I wasn't sure myself.

Julia sighed. 'Still think selling to CFC's a good idea?'

28

'Why the hell not. If there aren't any local objections –'

'There won't be,' Mrs Buckham interrupted. 'We've had yuppies, luppies and guppies since the eighties. A few more won't make any difference.'

Even Julia smiled indulgently.

'So, if there aren't any local objections,' I repeated, 'and the price is right, well, goodbye to the farm next door.'

Chapter 6

I had more post flopping through the door in the next
few weeks than I'd had in the previous two years.
Correspondence rocketed back and forth between
myself, the estate agent, my solicitor and Amy. I
was convinced I'd get RSI with all the form signing I had
to do.

AnnaMaria thought it was hysterical. Every time she
came home from work I was on the phone to my solicitor
attempting to fathom some legal loophole or other.

Mrs Buckham tried and failed to help with this, and
instead was starting to fret about her shop. The
gas man's one-week estimate had turned to two and,
she assured me, at the rate the builders were working
on the renovations, her stay could be extended by
another month.

Not, I suppose, that she wasn't useful. Once she got
the hang of the Aga and a meat-free household, she
cooked and presented meals with infuriating military
precision. Beds were made with boarding-house
efficiency; the sheets were so tight, a nun would have
been comfortable.

Sylvia shared her love and intimate knowledge of the

cinema with me. We sat through her favourite films; the half-dozen classics, that weren't now in storage, spanned as many decades. Mrs Buckham liked to measure her life to date in celluloid, starting with Chaplin's *The Great Dictator* and ending with *Titanic*, her favourite film of the nineties.

In between the film shows we caught up with the news, something I rarely watched, just enough to keep a foothold in the current century. She knew this, the whole village knew this but it was a fix Mrs Buckham needed to have nightly. At one particularly low point we viewed a news round-up of the previous half-decade or so. A stand up newswoman delivered a droll monologue observing that Bill Clinton, set to be a news item for the rest of his days and beyond, could have saved the lives of countless Iraqis if only he'd worn a condom. A leap of logic from a cynical Channel 4.

And just how far would taxpayers have to reach into their pockets to pay for the farce of the recent prison escapes? In a seemingly co-ordinated move, three prisons – one in Preston, a newly privatised one somewhere in the North East and Styal, the women's prison in Cheshire – had suffered a breakout by members of a team of armed robbers. There were no leads and no clues as to their whereabouts.

'Try Spain,' Mrs Buckham had informed the TV. 'They all end up there sooner or later. I remember this lot.' She stabbed a finger at the screen as their mug shots appeared. 'Vicious, they were. Even the woman.' She shook her head, disgusted and let down by a member of her sex.

I pointed out that the woman, Lorna something or other, had, as far as I could tell, only been the getaway driver.

'Don't you believe it. Look,' she commanded as the

Royal Thistle Bank's CCTV footage of the robbery flickered into view. It was the usual *Crimewatch* quality: ghostly and scratched, as though taken from a nearby planet.

Despite a lack of disguise – they all wore plain black trouser suits, gloves and matching baseball caps – I couldn't make out the age, the sex, or the race of the perpetrators. They could have been a gang of female Chinese pensioners as far as I was concerned.

But the crime was as vicious as Sylvia remembered. Although the stop/start footage obscured the worst of the offences, there was no getting round the appalling attack on two of the bank's officials. The newsreader explained that because of the beatings they'd received the assistant manager, a woman, had lost her sight in one eye; and the other victim, a teller, who had been forced to help load money into bags, was unlikely to work again.

Sylvia's obsession with the news and her videos was driving me ever so slightly round the twist. Her films were beginning to haunt me – her impersonation of di-Caprio clinging frozen to the lifeboat was faultless. I even considered giving the renovators a hand so as to get her out of my hair that bit quicker.

She was almost as annoying as my mother.

And speaking of mothers, Margaret Campbell had finally got in touch, after a silence lasting almost six weeks.

It's not very often I'm proved right, and I wasn't on this occasion either. But I wasn't far wrong.

The invitation for the engagement party was less than original. As would be the wedding invitation, to follow later in the year. A cream envelope contained a cream and silver embossed card. Formality was slavishly adhered to.

I could imagine the hours spent over the intricate dance of engagement plans. I could almost see the copy of Debrett's at one elbow. And a thesaurus at the other, in case she repeated herself.

There'd been an ancient copy of polite society's dos and donts at the library where Anne worked and she'd brought it home for a laugh once, but it had been nicked by someone with no social skills whatsoever. Scarily, after Sara Paretsky's novels, it was still Mum's favourite book.

There was a covering letter with the invite.

'I should have phoned, I know,' it began, dispensing with any other sort of greeting. 'Sorry, Letitia, I was afraid you'd try and talk me out of it.'

Why would I? Why should I? She was her own woman and in the last six months or so a wedding or engagement had clearly been on the cards. The notion of a stepfather wasn't that unattractive. And her fiancé-to-be was okay, if a bit batty in his old colonial ways.

There were three invitations in the envelope. One for me, one for Julia, and one for AnnaMaria, plus 'a guest' each should we wish to bring one. The shindig was to be held at the Colonel's home in Scotland. A hand-drawn picture of his estate – which had been in his family for generations – adorned the front of each card.

I'd never visited the place, though I'd been invited the previous year for Christmas celebrations. The thought had made my blood run cold. The Colonel was odd, but harmless. His relatives, on the other hand, sounded decidedly peculiar. Mum had told me some of their stories. The family's younger generation had interesting CVs ranging from speeding offences and drink driving to heroin dealing. The tales of life on the aristocratic edge were seedy and sickening, and, knowing AnnaMaria's views on such things, I doubted if she could be persuaded to go. No such problem with Julia. She wasn't averse to a bit of social climbing, whatever our hosts' background.

And I would have to go. With or without Debrett's, it would be poor form to turn down such an invitation from my mum.

The engagement party was set for late June, which didn't really give me much time to prepare. I'd have to organise cover for the farm and I wanted to settle the business with Amy before I swanned off. I decided to approach the sheep farmer already renting the land next door. Stan was an agreeable sort of bloke and the price I was charging him was nominal. I hoped he'd feel he owed me a favour anyway.

I rang him and he agreed to look after the hens for a long weekend. I promised him a rent-free period but warned him about the farm's imminent sale.

'Don't worry about that, Letty,' he said. 'The lambs'll be gone to the abattoir by then. It's time I got out of this game, there's no money in it nowadays, y'know, not like when I was a lad,' he grumbled, the same grumble he'd been uttering for years. 'But I can let you have a freezerful at half price if you want. Not much fat on them this year, the leg chops should be tasty and a couple of nice roasts for Sunday –'

I stopped him there and told him to offer it to Julia. Food and animals didn't have the same associations for her.

As I suspected, AnnaMaria declined the invite to Mum's do.

'Not that I don't want to go,' she said hastily, the following weekend. 'You know how I feel about

34

Margaret. Lovely woman, you should make more of an effort with her.' She stared through the kitchen window at Liam as he climbed in to the large chicken run. From my vantagepoint at the open kitchen door, I could see chicken feathers protruding at odd angles from his tangle of blond hair. Not for him the age-old game of cowboys and Indians. He was bright enough to understand AnnaMaria's descriptions of exploitation. And he was astute enough to play along. For him, there were Indians, and then there were other Indians, at least in front of his mum. Sometimes I felt I knew Liam better than she did.

'So why don't you come then?' I asked, ignoring the dig about my own mother.

'I don't really want to take Liam. I don't think I'd like the influences.'

I shifted in my chair to get a better look at her. 'Do you have to take him?'

She was silent, she'd not thought of that option. I laughed. 'Or do you think they'll be a bad influence on you, too?'

Suddenly she banged on the kitchen window. 'Liam! Off there, now.'

Liam dangled precariously from the single apple tree growing in the back garden. He shimmied down it as though his bones were made of rubber and his sinews of elastic. Safe at the base of the tree, he gave his mother a wave and shot an imaginary foe with an imaginary bow and arrow. Whooping, he chased the pullets in the general direction of the bottom fields where, finally, after putting it off for years, I'd planted rows and rows of organic autumn crops. Spuds, mostly. Winter boilers that would flourish in the well-drained peaty soil that had lain fallow for far too long. I planned to take them

35

to market once I'd harvested them in October.

'Don't trample the vegetables,' AnnaMaria called after her son.

'Oh, he'll do more good than harm,' I assured her. 'He'll keep the crows at bay, might even squash a few slugs while he's at it.'

AnnaMaria was thoughtful for a minute. 'Do you know, I think I will come along, after all. Mrs Buckham will probably look after Liam. Or Andy's mum. She says she doesn't see enough of him.'

I thought, but didn't say, that Andy's mum was still convinced she was Liam's real grandmother, not just an honorary one. Her expression of love when she'd last collected him for babysitting had confirmed it as far as I was concerned.

'Well actually,' I said, 'I was going to invite Mrs Buckham too.'

'Really?' AnnaMaria squeaked in surprise. After a moment she added, 'Why?'

'I thought she'd probably enjoy herself.'

Looking back, the word *enjoy* was ill considered.

Chapter 7

I hit Calderton ten days later. My appointment with my solicitor and CFC had finally arrived.

Apart from 'TV Technology', a video shop Mrs Buckham almost single-handedly kept in business, an off licence Julia seemed to have shares in, and a new fried chicken takeaway wickedly entitled 'Gobble and Go', the centre of Calderton village had only recently begun to leave the nineteen-fifties. A rare thing in West Yorkshire.

Where other villages had embraced change, my adopted home town had clung to an earlier, mythically friendlier age. The various shops, lining one main street, hadn't altered much in four decades. They'd been in and out of fashion at least twice since I'd moved here from Manchester. And since the nearest supermarket was too far away simply to 'drop-in', the local businesses continued to make a profit.

A traditional butcher's, with meat delivered straight from the local abattoir, did a roaring trade. The commuters who lived in the area had at first eschewed the home-made sausages, black puddings and sweet-cured bacon the shop specialised in. But as vegetarianism lost its trendy image, they flocked to buy Jim's ham shanks, his specially prepared offal, and lamb so young it had barely learned to bleat.

Other small enterprises did an equally brisk trade, perhaps simply because of this unwillingness to modernise. Two old ladies, with nearly a hundred and fifty years' experience between them, ran a haberdashery. With wool grown, spun and dyed locally, their colourful products were in great demand. They had a bit of a reputation, too. In the seventies they'd held out as long as they could against metrication. Maybe the suffragette somewhere in her family tree compelled Emily Green to chain herself to the Weights and Measures van.

Miss Green and her companion, Emily Ball, were having a hard time coping with the threat of a single currency. They'd probably go back to bartering. Half a cup of sugar for a needle and thread. A pound of lard for a couple of lace doilys. You get the idea.

Even more outrageous events had occurred in the village since, some of them, unfortunately, centred on me, but we'd be here for ever if I went into them now.

I passed the shop where the dangerous Emilys spent their days, and spied a colourful poster. It almost filled the central pane of the shop window, and it read:

EAST EUROPEAN AID CONVOY LEAVING CALDERTON SOON.

WANTED: WOOLLEN BLANKETS AND CHILDREN'S CLOTHES. ANY CONDITION.

PLEASE DEPOSIT AT TYRE AND TREAD GARAGE, HALIFAX ROAD. OR CAN COLLECT.

A contact number was printed below the main message. The poster didn't say who was doing the organising, but Calderton wasn't short of kindly souls, from Girl Guides to a shadowy Buddhist community situated a few miles out of town.

Thinking about it, AnnaMaria had bags of clothes that didn't fit Liam any more taking up space in her attic room. Maybe it was time I had a clearout, too. I was sure I'd seen a pile of blankets and sheets gathering dust in the garage.

I was finally to meet Chris F Crozier (by chance, on holiday from his beloved Texas), the head honcho of CFC, and new owner of East Brook Farm. I imagined he saw George's old place as just another feather in his cap, about as important to him as a second-hand PC was to Bill Gates.

Megan Jones, my solicitor, was a young, Calderton-born hard hitter. She'd had some experience and opportunities with law firms in larger towns but something – Sylvia reckoned near-bankruptcy – had brought her back to the village of her birth. The tedium of her job would have killed me. Conveyancing made chicken farming look as exciting as space travel.

The Jones & Company office had formerly been a three-storey weaver's cottage, as had many of the shops on the main road. Built a century and a half ago, its stone-fronted and blackened exterior was a last link to a dynamic industrial age that had finally petered out when the local train station had closed in the sixties. The line had been reopened ten years ago, but now the trains whizzed commuters rather than cotton or wool backwards and forwards. A pathetic exchange according to Mrs Buckham.

I parked my Land Rover across the street from the office. A few shoppers sauntered past. A purposeful young mother with a pram and a toddler in tow clattered along the pavement. A couple of teenage boys, bored as only teenagers can be, sat on a wall cradling skateboards. A conversation started up as I went past and I mentally tried to block their comments. 'Lezzy' – or was that 'Letty the Lezzy' – drifted my way. I glared. They glared back and then hooted with laughter as I crossed the road. Didn't they watch *Oprah*, or *Ricky Lake*?

'Get a life,' I called over my shoulder. They dissolved into laughter again.

Megan Jones had introduced a groovy new millennium feel to her company. None of this oak and leather for her. Plastic moulded chairs in startling blues and yellows lined the walls of the reception area, and an auburn-haired, shapely young woman in jeans and a zip-up cardigan sat behind a brushed steel desk. She looked familiar and I realised she had attended the same college as AnnaMaria, though they hadn't been on the same course. She tapped away at her trendy blue computer that matched the décor, of course. Otherwise, the office was empty.

I strolled across the lino; its colourful swirls and complex pattern would give me a headache in about ten seconds. It reminded me of a McDonald's, except that the hyperactive kids and estranged fathers with more money than sense were missing.

Megan Jones came bursting through the door behind me.

'Letty,' she bellowed in greeting. 'You're early. Sue, where are those files I asked you to get?'

Sue didn't look up. 'They've been on your desk for the last half-hour,' she replied languidly.

The soft tap-tap of rubber-coated keys on the plastic

keyboard filled the ensuing silence.

'Letty, do you want coffee?' Sue asked, still with her eyes glued to the screen.

'If it's no trouble,' I ventured.

'No trouble.'

Megan rushed past me and leaned over Sue's desk to look at the computer. 'What's this?' she asked.

'That letter you asked me to type five minutes ago.'

Tap-tap.

'Oh.'

'Letty, come through.' Megan looked flustered. She had a file jammed under her armpit.

The colour scheme, Megan's nerve-jangling behaviour and an impassive Sue were making me breathless. I followed Megan out of reception and into her large, multi-chaired office. Sue, somehow, had made coffee and was planting it before me just as I took a seat. She placed the letter she'd been typing on Megan's desk. Megan, meanwhile, had her back to me and was rooting through a five-door metal cabinet.

Sue silently left the room.

'Be with you in a mo,' Megan mumbled. Files were dragged from the cabinet and slung onto a chair. Without looking, she reached behind her for the office intercom.

'Sue, where's that letter?'

'On your desk.'

The intercom clicked off.

Megan used her hip to slam the drawer shut and then turned to me with a smile. 'You wouldn't think a receptionist could be too efficient, would you?' Finally, she took a seat.

Megan's office, thankfully, was a little more restful than the reception area, that is, if you could ignore the piles of paper scattered everywhere. It was also a bit hot and stuffy.

The walls were painted barleywhite, the ceiling was deep cream and the carpet was utility grey. Megan spotted me gazing around.

'I haven't had this room done yet. I thought orange. Hopefully I should be able to throw some money at the place before long,' she muttered, half to herself. 'Anyway, I've got your papers ready for signature. You've done well out of this, Letty. We lost eight thousand pounds on the asking price, as you know, but with today's market for farmland, that's not bad at all.' She thrust a file towards me. 'That's your copy to keep. I have the originals of course –'

The intercom buzzed.

'Chris Crozier and party are here,' Sue hissed hollowly.

'Just give me five minutes, Sue, then show them in.'

'And somebody's phoned about some blankets,' Sue went on.

'Yes, whatever,' Megan snapped.

I could hear Sue tut loudly before she snapped off the intercom. I looked at Megan's flushed face in surprise. 'Are you organising that?' I asked.

She smiled. 'Just co-ordinating it. As a favour.' She fanned her reddened complexion with her hand.

'I've got some bits and pieces you might be able to use. I'll drop them off.'

'Every little helps,' she said and got up to open the window. 'Is it stifling in here, or is it me?'

'It's stifling,' I agreed. My feet were on fire and I guessed Megan had left the underfloor heating on. Seeing her in action, it was just the sort of thing she'd do.

Megan returned to her seat and ran her hand over her

42

short dark hair. She wore a navy suit and a crisp white shirt, a small gold chain nestled against her skin. She might have been scatty but her makeup was immaculate, and dramatic. Berry-red lipstick and kohl-blackened eyes made her look slightly older than her thirty-five years.

'All I need now are signatures from those involved in the transaction,' she said, all business. 'A formality only, but a legal one. And of course your cheque. This could have been finalised through the post, but Chris was pretty insistent it was all done face to face. I'm so glad you don't mind. Chris Crozier is quite an imposing character.' She smiled again. There was a perfunctory knock at the door before it swung open to reveal a group of strangers.

'Ah, Ms Crozier, welcome,' Megan said.

Chris as in Christine the female offspring then, I thought as the Texan reached for Megan's hand.

I got a brisk and aggressive 'Hi there' from my new neighbour, and as everyone took their seats – Chris Crozier's attorney; a big bloke with no title called Lee; and, drifting in from the corridor, Amy – I took a second to assess Ms Crozier, and her entourage.

She was a small woman; younger than me, older than Megan, with dyed blonde hair – shoulder length, expensively styled – and she wore a yellow Texas Terriers' sweatshirt (whoever they were), and faded, close-fitting jeans. Unlike Megan, her face was free of makeup. Her skin was tanned and flawless and her accent was straight off the range. Think Dolly Parton on twenty Park Drive a day.

She immediately took charge of the proceedings.

'So where d'y'all want me to sign?' She aimed the question at me, with a smile.

'She's the lady to ask,' I said, waving a finger at Megan. The *lady*? Where did that come from?

Files were opened and Chris's attorney read the forms quickly and in silence before handing them over.

We scrawled our signatures, Sue was called in to witness, and everything was done and dusted within ten minutes.

I never expected to make so much money with so little effort. It was all slightly unreal.

'So,' Chris said, slapping her hands on her thighs. 'Where do you people eat around here?'

'The Grange,' Sue piped up decisively.

I looked at her leaning by the door and the mischievous grin she flashed was just for me.

'Hell, get your jackets then. The Grange it is. Lee, pass me the goddamned mobile.'

Nobody moved. 'That's all of you,' Chris said as Lee handed her the phone and Sue, without needing to be asked, rooted out the restaurant's number. 'You do eat in England, don't you?'

We did, of course, but not at the Grange.

Situated a few miles to the east, the Edwardian Grange Hotel was one of the snazzier places in Yorkshire. If not the snazziest. Set among tall, leafy oak trees, which were almost as old as the building itself, the Grange had been converted from some old boys' residence into a succesful hotel (the current owners had beat the National Trust's offer by a whisker). It was the sort of place occasionally used as a setting for BBC costume dramas. The food was supposed to be pretty good. Guest chefs were always making an appearance and Jilly Goolden, that doyenne of wine tasters, had quaffed a few bottles there once upon a time.

I knew the maître d' at the Grange – I'd had egg

dealings with him in the past. Usually closeted and anxious, Vince Mumford had last crossed my path at a bar in Manchester during the Mardi Gras. Or at least his alter ego had. I'd hardly recognised him. From formal black suit to skimpy ripped shorts (clinging tenaciously below the belt line) in one easy gay lesson. Round of face and round of belly, his black skin was rippled, rather than ripped; more of a max pack than a six pack. His admiring boyfriend was all over him. Surprisingly, Vince had said hello and we'd even had a bit of a chat about being queer and, in his case, black in Calderton.

He probably felt he was safe in the knowledge that, as his least likely customer, I'd never pass through the doors of the Grange. Maybe that was unfair, we'd soon see.

Chris Crozier, with softly chuckled words and enough Texan charisma to fill an oil well, had managed to book a table for five.

'You boys have work to do today,' Chris informed her employees as she handed the phone back to Lee. They were obviously familiar with this type of treatment; briefcases and papers were gathered together without a word. 'I want to get to know Letty a bit better. Let's start as we mean to go on.'

She put an arm round me and squeezed. I wasn't sure if I'd get used to this touchy feely stuff. Old George, my former neighbour, wouldn't have prodded me with the rough end of a yard brush. Mind you, I would rather have bathed in cow dung than lay my hands on his unsavoury person.

Releasing me, she went outside for a quick business huddle with the boys. Amy went to the toilet and I got a private moment to relieve Megan of a pretty substantial cheque. I'd managed to avoid paying inheritance tax; the cheque was substantial but not *that* substantial, and the

45

enforced drop in price had ensured a distinct lack of interest from the local tax inspector.

Megan shepherded us outside as she locked up her offices. We didn't get a taxi. We didn't get a bus either. Instead Chris Crozier showed a certain skill behind the wheel of a big black Ford Senator. Even with one arm propped on the open window, she didn't waver across to the wrong side of the road once.

'I do love these little lanes of yours,' she said as we hit a short stretch of motorway.

Chris caught my pursed look and roaring with laughter, slapped my unsuspecting thigh. Petite she may have been but her hands were like a navvy's.

Sue giggled but Chris's knowing glance at me suggested that her facetiousness was deliberate. I wasn't sure what to make of this loud and generous woman at all.

Megan, who'd been unwilling to leave the office for an unexpected lunch – unexpected to me, too, but 'no' wasn't an answer Chris was used to hearing – was studying papers, oblivious to the conversation. Obviously she couldn't afford to snub a wealthy client but her face was a picture. Amy sat in silence at the back of the car; I guessed her career was too important for her to even think about a refusal. Sue, though, was simply looking forward to something a bit more inspiring than the bakery's traditional offerings. Striking that this little Texan woman could have so much power over such formidable women.

Chris yakked on all the way to the Grange. We got a colourful description of her ranch, her State and the brisk business her various interests enjoyed.

CFC Inspirational Health and Beauty, to give it its full title, was but one small pie in one great big oven.

'Honey,' she said to me, 'I'd just get bored if I didn't have all this,' and she waved her arm as though Yorkshire was part of her empire too. 'My daddy gave me the idea, as well as the financial backing,' she added with a half whisper. 'A dynamic man, he's very familiar with the Brits, visits as often as he can. He has so many friends and so many concerns in this little country of yours, you wouldn't believe it.' She laughed. 'Anyway, he told me to get over here and help him out.' She paused. 'And I expect you to come callin' to the Croziers' new venture. I'll get you a discount.' I got another slap on the thigh. 'You could do with a good facial, honey, your complexion's getting that farming look. And we're licensed for the odd nip and tuck, if you want to take advantage of our surgeon's skills. Now look at my skin, never neglected it, don't expect to see a wrinkle for twenty years.'

It took me a moment or two to realise that I'd been insulted.

'You still want a man to come knocking at your door? Am I right, or am I right?' She took her eyes off the road for a second and gave me a look that I couldn't even begin to fathom.

I opened my mouth and shut it quickly as Amy sneaked an unseen hand around the back of my seat and gripped me firmly above the elbow. Pins and needles shot down my arm to my fingertips. I turned to glare at her as Chris's gaze returned to the road. That pinch, a stern look and a quick shake of the head stopped the 'Actually, I'm gay' comment that Amy, somehow, had guessed was coming.

I hardly knew Amy. God, I didn't know any of them really, yet she felt she had the right to stop me in my verbal tracks. What business was it of hers?

I needed an explanation, and I needed one fast.

The moment passed, though, and we were back to a commentary on the pleasures and problems of running CFC as Chris followed Megan's pointed directions to the Grange.

Vince Mumford steered us past crowded tables, with pleasant words to us all, but without a word about our attire. He exuded a recently acquired customer-service warmth and he was neither overtly camp nor unduly starched. His amiable, relaxed manner was more café-bar than stately home.

The décor had also made concessions to café society: in place of elaborate curtains, cotton blinds let in gentle summer sunshine. The walls of the restaurant were colour washed and the lighting was bright, cheerful and chic. I'd expected oak and polished brasses, candelabras and snotty waiters.

The contemporary look hadn't quite extended to the French-influenced menu, and though the Grange didn't yet enjoy any Michelin stars, I had noticed a glass frame full of positive reviews from the Sunday supplement.

We perused the menu in silence.

'Fish stew, eh?' Sue remarked suddenly. 'Or bangers and mash.'

I looked carefully, scanning for these commonplace dishes. Potato Rosti and herb and garlic Cumberland slices with Chef's special sauce was obviously the latter, but fish stew? Perhaps the mullet in mussel and prawn . . . something incomprehensible . . . in French.

I skipped to the vegetarian choice as restaurant life hummed on around us.

Some choice – another Gallic thing that I assumed was mushroom omelette, or a cheese-based meal that sounded suspiciously like Welsh Rarebit at a price Gary Rhodes would have found obscene. Despite the hefty cheque in my pocket, I was glad I wasn't paying.

We ordered.

And waited.

Chris Crozier filled the gaps.

In that twenty minutes I learned more about Texas than I ever would have wished to. It should have been fascinating, but somehow it wasn't. Her bird's eye view was from the sort of wealthy platform most people could never even imagine.

No poverty in the Lone Star State, then?

The glorified cheese on toast filled a huge dinner plate and the side salad that came with it would have kept a rabbit going for a week. Sprigs of fresh herbs littered the edge of the plate and intricately patterned tomatoes added a little colour. It was about as good as cheese on toast could get.

I reached for my cutlery. Enough surrounded me to fill my knife and fork drawer. I knew the saying 'work from the outside in'; I wasn't dragged up, after all. But so much silverware made that rule seem redundant.

So, which to choose?

Who cares?

I took the bluntest knife and a fork that didn't look as though it would spear a tonsil every time I took a mouthful.

'A moment, honey, please,' Chris interrupted before I had a chance to attack the food.

What followed embarrassed me more than any inability to choose the right accoutrements.

Chris lowered her head.

Prayers before lunch, with lots of 'bless us' and 'thank you, Lord'.

I wanted to crawl under the table. Sue gazed into the distance, irritably mauling a napkin. Megan looked as uncomfortable as I felt but Amy, to my utter surprise, was deep in prayer.

I could tell that this lunch was going to be hard work.

Chapter 8

I'd never been so pleased to arrive back in Calderton. Even the two teenage monsters, still lurking by my Land Rover, were agreeable company after a couple of hours with Chris F Crozier.

How many weird women could I meet in a lifetime? It had started with my mother, and my new neighbour had just edged the number into double figures. Maybe it was me. Intolerance had begun to show with the departure of my lover and the arrival of my last birthday. At this rate I'd be voting Tory by the time I hit fifty.

Why should I care about someone's religious beliefs? Sita's faith was still strong and Mrs Buckham's friend Amna, who worked at the local cash and carry, would quote from the Koran at the shake of a prayer mat. Even Sylvia Buckham pinched bits from every religion known to humanity when she wanted to be on unimpeachable ground. And I'd met so many women of the cloth when Anne had been researching her first biblically based tome not to be shocked by anything.

But this Southern Baptist fire that Chris seemed so fond of had licked around my feet long enough to make me feel uncomfortable. I tried to tell myself it was a

51

personal choice. But the reason that Amy had stopped me from explaining my sexuality was clear.

My intolerance? Why should I worry?

I thrust the thoughts aside. Chris Crozier was opening a health farm, not the Temple of Doom. You didn't need to pray to use an exercise bike.

I'd been dropped off at the end of the street with a, 'See ya later, honey,' still ringing in my ears. I passed Sylvia Buckham's corner shop as I hurried towards my Land Rover and I couldn't resist a quick glimpse inside. The front door was open slightly although the gas work was finished, as was obvious from the shiny new copper pipes skirting the walls and the absence of the appropriate van. It was also clear that the guts of the place had been ripped out. The much talked about renovation was in full swing. Smashed concrete lay underfoot and bits of planking littered the ground. I stepped gingerly onto my old friend's premises and, from the direction of the kitchen at the back, I could hear nails being plied from wood. The place was full of sawdust and it was making my nose itch. Suddenly I sneezed: a noisy, wet explosion. The shriek of metal on wood continued for a moment. There was the sound of something scraping across the floor and the soft fall of footsteps. I tried to shout a warning 'hello' – I had no qualms about being on Sylvia's property, but it only seemed polite – and then I sneezed again, louder than ever.

I needed a tissue desperately and had just rammed it up my nostrils when a figure wearing white overalls and clutching a hammer suddenly appeared around the corner of the newly plastered wall. I took a step back in surprise but the other person was clearly as startled as me and we simply stared at each other for a moment.

'Hello,' I managed, stuffing the snotty tissue into the back pocket of my jeans.

The figure lowered the hammer. A mouth moved beneath a crisscross of bandages and a faintly snuffly but definitely female voice said, 'Who are you?' Her eyes carefully locked on to my face.

I took a breath. 'I'm Letty, a friend of Sylvia's. Are you doing the conversion?'

'Just lending a hand with the floorboards,' she said, sweeping a baseball cap from her head. She proceeded to scratch her head with the sort of enthusiasm that would have had the most vicious canine kicking its legs in ecstasy. Short, bright red hair sprang around her bandages. I tried, but couldn't drag my eyes away from her damaged face. I had no idea who she was. Despite the dressings, I would have recognised the voice and certainly the hair. 'You're not local?' I queried.

'No,' she said and smiled a small, tight smile. She grimaced, presumably at the pain and not at me.

I was suddenly embarrassed. 'I just saw the door open and ... well, I suppose I was a bit concerned. Sylvia's staying with me at the moment you see.'

The woman paused to gingerly touch her nose. She winced again.

'And you are?' I pressed.

She crunched the baseball hat into her fist. 'Liz. Sorry, I'm Liz.' Releasing the hat from a stranglehold, she held out a leather-gloved hand for me to shake. She was taller than me, lean and wiry.

'Excuse the bandage,' she sniffled. 'An accident,' and she looked accusingly at the hammer. Perhaps she'd been banging nails in with her head. Strange thought.

'Well, I'd better get on.' With a gesture I realised she

was completely unconscious of, she flicked the hammer into the air. It spun three times, wood and metal blurring in the dim light before she caught it backhanded. It slapped heavily in her palm. I had another idea as to where she might have got her injuries. 'Bye then,' she snuffled. I smiled faintly and stepped back across the shop floor and out onto the street.

The strange encounter was soon forgotten when I checked my watch. I'd arranged to go with AnnaMaria to the new playschool she had in mind for Liam. She thought – though I've no idea why – that I would be a good influence on the Principal. If I looked sharp I'd still be able to get to the meeting. AnnaMaria'd kill me if I was late.

But all of the gods were suddenly against me.

From a distance of twenty yards it was clear I had a flat tyre. Great, another delay.

The two teenagers came roaring down the street on their skateboards. I readied myself for more insults.

'Weren't us,' the taller of the two yelled unexpectedly as he flashed past me.

'Ya can't blame us,' the second insisted. His black curly hair was unfashionably long and reached past his shoulders. He had a hank of it twined between his fingers as he leaped from the kerb onto the road just inches from my toes. His golden skin was flawless, not a teenage spot in sight, and his eyelashes were long and as black as his hair.

I turned to look at him, disconcerted for some reason by his prettiness. He looked worried but not exactly guilty.

'What?' I asked.

He exchanged a glance with his friend. Some silent communication passed between them. Back on the pavement they skated around me. His companion, with a precision that would have once made him an electrician's – or, given Liz's party piece, maybe a joiner's – apprentice, flipped the edge of his skateboard with his foot and caught it one-handed. He tucked it under his elbow and strode towards me, baggy carpenter jeans and enormous hooded sweatshirt flapping around his gangly body. His hair was shaved at the sides, close to his nobbly skull.

'It weren't us,' he stated, brown eyes defiantly holding mine. He swiped the beginnings of a dreadlocked fringe from his eye.

'Have I blamed you?' I asked, realising that abuse wasn't about to come my way.

'Well, people blame us for all sorts,' the younger of the two said. 'Don't they, Gaz?'

'Too right, Darren,' was the serious reply.

There was a long pause as I checked the damaged tyre.

'We saw you go off with that Yank and that posh bird,' Gaz informed me.

Posh bird? He meant Megan.

'Yeah,' Darren interrupted, black eyes glittering. 'Where were you off to, like?'

'Shush, Darren,' his mate snapped.

Darren was quiet for a minute and then retorted, 'Yer went to the Grange, didn't you?'

'How the hell do you know?'

'Vince is me cousin, three times removed. He rang me mobile. Honest to God, he's such a gossipy old queen. I always reckon it's who you know not what you know, innit?' he said coyly.

'We'll help you fix the tyre,' Gaz joined in. 'Cost you though.'

'Depends how long it takes,' I said, amazed at the turn

the conversation had taken. The word privacy should be stricken from all of Calderton's dictionaries. 'A fiver if you do it in ten minutes.' I knew it would take me much longer on my own.

'Each?' Darren said hopefully.

'Between you.'

A muttered debate ensued.

'Deal,' Gaz said. He held out his hand to shake mine. 'Sorry about earlier,' he went on quietly. 'Didn't mean nothing. We call Vince queer all the time. He never seems to mind.'

I shrugged, gripped his bony hand briefly and went about the business of removing the spare tyre.

The Land Rover was jacked up and the flattened tyre removed in less than five minutes. I examined it when Gaz and Darren rolled it towards me. A bloody big nail just above the rim had done the damage.

AnnaMaria was waiting on the doorstep when I finally got home, Liam's hand firmly clutched in her own and Mrs Buckham peering over her shoulder. She dashed outside to greet me, dragging her son along, as I pulled up.

'Sorry I'm late,' I began.

'Letty,' Liam shrieked. 'I did this for you.' He pushed a piece of paper into my hands.

'Never mind the time,' AnnaMaria went on as though Liam hadn't spoken. 'I rang Mrs Scott to tell her we were behind schedule. What the fuck's going on next door?' she asked waving an arm wildly in the air. 'They started this almost as soon as you were out the door. Sylvia's been going mad with the noise.'

'It's enough to wake the dead,' Sylvia herself confirmed.

I glanced at the picture Liam had given me. The

slightly surreal image of a chicken on a tightrope (in a style Salvador Dali might have developed if he'd taken lessons from Lowry) gave me pause for thought. I promised the little boy I'd put it in a frame as soon as I could. His smile would have broken the hardest heart.

I looked across the way. Lorries had already arrived on the neighbouring farm. Fence posts and concrete bases were being delivered. The contractors' engines must have been revving up before the ink was even dry on the contracts.

'Oh well, I imagine we'll get used to it,' I said. 'I can't start complaining now, can I?'

'Got the dosh then?' AnnaMaria asked, laughing suddenly.

I tapped my back pocket and could feel the outline of the cheque. 'Oh, yes. Champagne tonight, I think.'

We watched the lorries start to offload as we climbed back into my vehicle.

'Less of a health farm, more like a fortress,' AnnaMaria observed as I slipped the Rover into first.

I explained the reason for my delay as we drove back to Calderton.

'Darren and Gaz?' AnnaMaria asked. 'Long black hair, killer good looks? The other's got weird looking dreads?'

I nodded.

'I know those two little sods. They're always hanging around the garage. Darren's dad's the one that owns that blue Cadillac. I wouldn't be surprised if they knackered your tyre for the fiver you gave them. Too soft, you.'

'I suppose so, but they're not so bad when you give them a chance ...'

'Yeah,' AnnaMaria said sourly. 'Right.'

57

Chapter 9

Three weeks later and my nerves were in tatters. I'd even begun to look forward to Mum's big do.

The view from the front porch and both front bedrooms had been changed for ever. No longer could the eye wander, unhindered, to the horizon. Blocks of six-foot, waney-lap fencing, treated in a golden colour that nature had never intended, were erected from one end of the farmyard to the other. The Berlin Wall couldn't have been more effective.

My chores finished for the day, I headed back to my house, unable to take the short route home. The track that had been shared by me and my neighbour no longer existed. Strictly speaking, George had owned the track, but we'd both used it for so long that it had never been an issue.

Until now.

There wasn't much I could do, or even say. I'd used the short cut with my old neighbour's permission and though my aunt had improved it, after a fashion, it wasn't common land. It was clearly shown on the plans as being part of the property I'd recently sold.

Still, consultation would have been nice.

★

Amy was watching Mrs Buckham pirouetting around the kitchen when I finally arrived home. Sylvia was showing off the new suit she'd bought for Mum's engagement do.

I'd managed to steer her away from some of the more inappropriate outfits that she'd spotted in her catalogue, but despite the broad choice of sizes – from 12 to 24 with Mrs Buckham somewhere in the middle – the selection of styles for this type of expedition was limited. And though I was the last person to want to see Sylvia back in old lady's clothes, she really needed a nudge in the right direction.

So AnnaMaria offered her help. Clothes weren't really her thing – that would be Julia, but her tastes were beyond most people's pockets – but she did have an eye for colour and style. In the end, the outfit that Sylvia had settled on appealed to both the eye and the budget.

The plum-coloured cotton trouser suit had been delivered earlier in the week. Sylvia had kept trying it on, any hapless visitor got an impromptu fashion show, and at the rate she was going the suit would be worn out before we got to Scotland.

'It's like it's made to measure,' she was saying delightedly. 'Just look at the detail,' she added, pulling on a gold button to prove her point.

'It's lovely,' Amy, her captive audience, replied earnestly.

'Hello,' I said warily.

'Ooh, Letty, I can't wait for the engagement party,' Mrs Buckham enthused.

Amy got to her feet as Sylvia dashed upstairs to get changed.

I smiled at Amy, though it felt a bit forced.

She smiled back, a little uncomfortable.

'Could I have a word?' she asked. 'I know it's all started rather quickly, the building work, that is ...'

Suddenly I was annoyed with her. I hadn't seen her for a couple of weeks but I was still angry with her about the incident on the way to the Grange and the fact that she'd not told me the date Chris was due to begin transforming the farm.

'I could have done with some warning. The hens have been in a state.'

I knew how stupid this sounded.

Amy, as twitchy as Mrs Buckham, fiddled with the collar of her silk blouse. I got a glimpse of a gold cross. 'I did ask her to give it some time. But she has deadlines, clients to attract. You know how it is. All the big papers and magazines are carrying adverts already. She's had a terrific response.'

I shrugged; my irritation still with me. I tried to shake it off. Chris Crozier was Amy's client and Chris now owned East Brook Farm. She was only doing what she had promised. Admittedly, a bit quicker than I had thought humanly possible. Still, I'd seen Barrett boxes being chucked up in neighbouring areas at an unbelievable speed so perhaps I shouldn't have been quite so surprised.

I filled the kettle.

'Anyway,' Amy went on. 'The basic alterations will be finished by next week. There hasn't been as much to do as you might imagine. Hopefully the noise won't be a problem by the time you get back from Scotland.'

I looked at her.

'Mrs Buckham explained,' she added hastily. 'Chris has asked me to invite you to the opening a week on Friday if you can make it –'

'It'll be completely finished by then?' I asked, amazed.

'Well, no. There will probably still be things that need to be done. She needs to landscape the gardens and will want to make sure the horses are suitably housed –'

'Horses?'

'Part of the health routine. Some of her clients expect it. With her being from Texas.'

I laughed and Amy looked relieved. 'So, she can expect you next Friday then?'

'I don't know. Will I be welcome?'

Her relieved look changed to one of puzzlement. 'Why wouldn't you be?'

'Amy,' I said, trying to hide my exasperation. 'You do know I'm gay?'

'So?' she said, guileless.

I reached for her arm and gripped her elbow. I didn't bother with an explanation.

'Oh, that,' she said, suddenly awkward. 'Chris can be a bit strange about certain things. I think her evangelical upbringing may have been quite strict.'

'And yours?' This was weird country. I'd met Amy only a couple of times. My initial feelings of warmth were cooling nicely.

Amy looked uncomfortable and she fidgeted again with her collar. 'Not strict, my upbringing, or evangelical. But we were Baptists just the same. I suppose the restaurant thing was just habit.' Her tone was almost, but not quite, apologetic.

Habit? You lose habits, especially if they don't mean anything to you.

'So, having a gay neighbour would get to her?'

'Why? Does having a Baptist neighbour get to you?' Needled, she tossed the question back at me.

I wanted to say no, it bloody well doesn't, but of course that would have been a lie.

We bristled at each other through the silence that followed.

Amy finally grabbed her handbag, that fresh, youthful look contorted by anger. 'I don't know you very well Letty, but I didn't think you'd be so prejudiced.'

I stared at her. I couldn't believe I was hearing this.

'Friday then? The offer's still open,' she spat.

'Wouldn't miss it,' I growled. I mentally planned my outfit. Nothing less than full drag. I'd flirt with the hostess, and announce my lesbianism from a tabletop.

Frostily, Amy bid me farewell and I took great pleasure in slamming the door on her departing back.

Bitch!

I repeated the strange conversation to Julia. I should have known better than to expect support.

It was Thursday, the evening before our trip to Scotland, and she'd invited me to tea at the Frog and Bucket, my local pub.

'I always thought you were more tolerant than that,' Julia announced, niftily scooping spaghetti. That trick with the spoon and fork always defeated me.

'I am tolerant,' I declared, though I was beginning to doubt it more and more.

'It's no fun, falling out with your neighbours.'

'Amy, thank God, is not my neighbour,' I retorted. My own pasta skittered from my spoon back onto my plate. I took a knife to it and chopped it into pieces.

'She'll report back though, won't she?'

'I don't know, and I care even less,' I replied angrily. 'Anyway, why should I bother? We've spent years fighting this kind of shit. I'm not going to crawl back into the closet for the likes of them.' Spaghetti splattered onto my trousers. 'Fuck,' I muttered. 'I was going to travel in these.'

'Calm down, for God's sake. Different strokes and all that,' Julia said. She grabbed the last piece of garlic bread and ran it around her plate. 'Don't let it get to you. I'm Catholic. That's never mattered to you.'

'Julia, you're as much a Catholic as the nearest yeti!'

Julia roared. 'Oh, Letty,' she spluttered. 'Don't let my mother hear you say that. Or bang goes my inheritance. It's taken her years to get used to the idea of me being a dyke –'

'Only because it took you years to tell her. If you hadn't 've got involved with Sita, she'd still be guessing.'

Julia, unruffled, sat back in her chair. 'So what's really bothering you, then?' she asked, lighting a cigarette.

'How do you mean?'

Julia leaned forward, elbowing plates aside. 'You don't really expect cults and weirdos, do you?'

I didn't reply at first, merely watched smoke curl towards a yellowing ceiling. And then I grinned, probably at my own paranoia. 'Yeah, David Koresh's mother and Charlie Manson's sister boiling frogs and poisoning the water supply.'

'Margaret Thatcher's love child and the spawn of the devil taking over the world. Calderton, hot bed of sin and vice. An evil empire that will last for a thousand years!' Julia suggested with a Hitchcockian growl.

We giggled together quietly as the bar staff looked on. My fears were safely pigeon-holed, at least for the time being.

'Do you want pudding?' Julia asked at last.

'No, I'm stuffed. You can get me a beer though.'

Julia went to the bar and I glanced around the crowded pub. A food licence had been the Frog and Bucket's saviour. Newcomers to Calderton had lost the knack of going to the pub, and as cappuccino and latte bars gained ground in other areas, serious drinking had dwindled. The pub grub had been such a success that the education authority had hired Hilda, the sparklingly professional landlady, to supply local schools with dinners. They were the best-fed kids for twenty miles.

Julia came back with two pints of Watmough's Special Anti-Gravity Bitter, the local speciality. 'By the way, I asked Sita to come along to Scotland, but she hasn't got the time so I invited my mother instead.' She paused, waiting for a reaction. I remained silent. 'I think I probably left it a bit late for her to make arrangements though. You know what she's like. It takes her for ever to organise Dad.'

'Why? He's not ill, is he?'

'No, just awkward. Anyway, I've not heard anything, so . . .' She shrugged and left the sentence unfinished. 'It's a pity really.'

'What is?'

She took a slug of her beer. 'That Mum probably won't be there.'

'Why?' I asked.

'Your money, of course.'

Of course.

'Investments, international speculation, the money markets, FTSE, Dow Jones. What she doesn't know could be written on the back of a cheque.'

'It's already in my Building Society account,' I explained, not in the least surprised by her suggestion.

'Oh, Letty –'

'Never mind, "Oh, Letty". I know where it is, what it's doing and how fast I can get my hands on it. You are worse than my solicitor. Even my mother's got more sense than to make a fuss.'

'Yes, but Building Society? I didn't think there were

any left. And just imagine what you could earn if –'

'Not interested, Julia. It's safe, it's ethical –'

'And it's boring,' she interrupted.

I put my finger to my lips to silence her.

'Are you going to spend *any* of it?' she asked at last.

I was, and I explained that I was planning to buy AnnaMaria the Suzuki jeep she'd been hankering after.

'So that's why it's still stuck at the garage! I was ready to get rid of it. You do know the price?' she added carefully, a long, well-groomed finger toying with her hair. Her grey eyes appraised mine. We were clearly on her turf.

I swallowed more beer. 'There's always room for manoeuvre.' I grinned and offered an alternative figure to the asking price. She blustered and complained, and I had to endure a few low blows in the guilt department, but I knew I had her.

'I'll sort it out for you.' She relented, finally. 'I'll get Andy to take a look at it while we're in Scotland. It should be ready when we get back.'

'It's our secret till then,' I insisted.

We shook hands on the deal, finished our drinks and left the pub.

Chapter 10

We'd discussed the options regarding our trip up north. My Land Rover was sturdy and reliable, but noisy, elderly and uncomfortable. Julia was going in her MGF, no matter what, but it was a two-seater so we really needed something else as well. We could have hired another vehicle, could even have gone on the train but Julia, in an unaccustomed act of generosity, offered to lend me a four-wheel-drive Range Rover from the garage.

'Try it,' she urged. 'It's got more extras than Concorde. Ferocious wipers, heated windscreen, back and front, and a cabin heater that would have kept Scott's party alive. And the colour! Maroon and silver, you'll love it.' But my Land Rover, more familiar and with no hidden strings attached, was the vehicle I settled on.

The only outstanding problem was, who would travel with whom?

Julia and AnnaMaria on a four-hour journey together, alone? I don't think so. Mrs Buckham then? Even less likely.

So, I handed my car keys over to AnnaMaria. She

could cope with Mrs Buckham's ravings and I could handle Julia. Mrs Buckham would probably sleep most of the way anyway.

Stan arrived to oversee my livestock and take charge of the farm at six on Friday morning, and June – the honorary grandma – appeared an hour later to relieve AnnaMaria of Liam. By nine, we were ready to roll. As we swept out of the yard we passed the postie, who was clutching a bundle of letters. Bills, I thought – no need to stop for those!

Shortly after twelve we'd crossed the border.

Once we'd left the main highway and the lines of caravans heading northwards, I presumed, for a weekend break, we saw very little traffic.

I cracked open my window and the air was as different from the familiar smells of my farm as it could possibly get. Well, unless I went to India or China, or somewhere equally as exotic. Not much traffic perhaps, but plenty of wildlife. Fallow deer, which I recognised from *Wildlife On One* – any deer I'd seen in Calderton were usually already dead and cut into chunks on the butcher's slab – and the odd flash of an upturned rabbit's tail.

'Future roadkill,' Julia commented.

'You're just sick sometimes, Julia,' I told her.

'Well,' she retorted. 'Bunny rabbits and Bambi. What next for God's sake?'

I opened my window wider. 'Sniff,' I ordered.

Freshly scented air filled the tiny cockpit. Julia breathed deeply, and reached for her cigarettes.

'Disinfectant,' she stated, removing a fag from the packet and lighting it deftly. 'Like my toilet with a new blue-loo just thrown in.'

'Sad, Julia. You're just so sad.'

She smiled through the fog and opened her own window. Despite the bright sunshine, the hairs on my bare arms prickled and I shivered. The Scottish air was clearer and colder than the Yorkshire climate I was used to. In fact, everything was clearer. The sky, the endless array of tree tops that dominated the horizon. That was the major difference. Trees. Too many to count, enough to keep me in Christmas spruces for at least five lifetimes. Ten lifetimes. Maybe twenty.

Any doubts that we were on the right road were set aside. Mum had told me I would recognise the beginnings of the Colonel's estate because it was full of Norwegian spruce, forming a tree-lined gateway into the acres of property he and his family owned. Apparently the estate was famous for cultivating trees which weren't native to the area. We could have been in Canada, it was so un-British.

Mum had hinted that the forest was some sort of tax concession, though there were supicions that it did little for the Scottish environment. I could believe the tax concession theory and didn't really care what the trees were doing to the soil – Chris Crozier could stick Texas. I couldn't imagine anything quite as majestic as this scenery.

Julia, warmly dressed in a white Arran jumper and linen trousers (not, thankfully, in tartan), pointed at a distant double gate. 'Is that our turn?'

I grabbed the map from the dash and checked the road.

'Yep, that's us. Are they still behind us?'

Julia checked her mirror. 'Mmm,' she confirmed, didn't bother signalling, and swung left.

I glanced over my shoulder and watched as AnnaMaria overshot the turn. I heard a shriek of brakes and a throaty, diesel-driven growl as she reversed back up the road and finally followed us onto the side road. She flicked her headlights on and off irritably.

'Julia, you're just bad through and through.'

She cackled. 'That's me! Sad, bad and mad!'

The winding road took us closer to the fir trees that had so caught my breath, and on to parkland also owned by the Colonel's family. We drove over several cattle grids, though I couldn't see any cattle, past miniature lakes and not so miniature geese that honked and flapped at our cavalcade. Dogs barked in the distance and a flash of brown overhead announced the swift departure of half a dozen pheasants.

'Is it hunting season up here?' Julia asked.

'How the hell should I know?'

'Only asking,' she said, taking both hands off the steering wheel to make defensive gestures. 'I'm hardly likely to run out with a twelve bore and start blasting now, am I?'

'Sorry,' I said. 'I'm just a bit nervous.'

'Don't be,' Julia commanded. 'We're going to your mother's engagement party, not an execution. It's not as though she's asked you to be a bridesmaid or anything.'

'Julia! Don't even joke about that.'

Chapter 11

'Margaret, no!' I hissed.

We were in the garden. Well, garden might not quite be the right word.

Think garden for a moment. Little square lawn, a border of plants if you're lucky, or else the soil's so dead it poisons everything. A clothes line strung from end to end, sheets blowing in the wind.

Now think the absolute opposite: Sweeping acres of grassland; bushes cut into replicas of wildlife, huge oversized replicas that looked ready to bite your head off. It was big and it was impressive, if a bit predictable. A few billowing sheets might not have been such a bad addition.

'No,' I said again, as emphatically as I could when faced with maternal pressure.

'Letitia, please. Just think about it,' my mum, soon to be engaged to the owner of all I surveyed, begged.

Julia had been so wrong.

Me. A bridesmaid for God's sake!

And Julia, too, just for good measure.

'It won't be for at least six months. You can wear whatever you like,' she promised. 'Within reason,' she added after a thoughtful moment.

Who was this woman? She'd never pleaded in her life.

'Come on,' she said, taking my arm. 'Let's go for a walk.'

We wandered across a couple of hundred acres of lawn until we came to a gazebo, some glass and beech construction designed to protect those caught in the unpredictable Scottish weather.

Sunshine had greeted our arrival, quickly followed by squally showers and a chill, easterly wind. If I was ever going to wear thermal underwear, now would be the time. The Yorkshire climate may be changeable, but Scotland had the edge in the sort of pure, rugged, dramatic weather nineteenth-century writers were so fond of describing.

Mum had looked strangely out of place, clutching her umbrella, on the steps of the Colonel's nine-bedroomed family home. The soaring brickwork, gargoyles and gothic-inspired architecture dwarfed her. Still, I suppose that was the whole point of a place like this. It was supposed to remind the plebs of their station in life. A great big statement about who was in charge.

Julia was out of the car almost before the wheels stopped turning. It wasn't such a culture shock for her. The ostentatious wealth her family enjoyed had prepared her for anything Colonel Thompson's lot could throw at her.

Mum had greeted us alone, making a great play at Julia's affections. Not hard to do, really. If Mum ever decided she was a born-again lesbian and Sita persuaded herself that Julia wasn't worth the effort, I knew exactly whose knickers Julia would be trying to get into.

Crude, I know, but true.

'Margaret,' Julia said, kissing Mum's cheek. 'You look wonderful.'

Mum was pleased, natch.

'Decided on a date for the big day yet?'

To me, Mum's reply of 'Christmas, perhaps,' seemed a bit strained.

The welcome hug she gave AnnaMaria was genuine and the one she offered me was warm enough I suppose. She was even polite to Mrs Buckham who, as I'd predicted, had slept most of the way. Her grey hair stood out in a wild frizz. Overawed, and still half-asleep, she didn't utter a word.

'Where is everybody?' I'd asked as we extracted bags and presents from the back of the Land Rover.

'Doing something unmentionable to the wildlife, probably,' AnnaMaria whispered into my ear as we struggled with Mrs Buckham's extraordinary amount of luggage.

'They'll be back for dinner,' was all Mum said.

AnnaMaria and I had exchanged a glance. We both knew her well enough to know that things weren't quite right.

'Nerves,' AnnaMaria decided and added ominously, 'She should try driving your Land Rover for four hours. Test anybody's nerves that thing. Remind me to give it a going over when we get back. I've been on Dodgems less sluggish. When was the last time you had it serviced?'

I laughed. 'You should know,' I reminded her. 'You're the only person to have tinkered with it for the last, what, five years?'

She didn't answer burdened as she was by a large and a particularly awkward looking suitcase. 'How long does Sylvia think she's stopping?' she wheezed, as she slung it up the steps.

The party, guided by black-suited staff, had been left to settle into their rooms, while Mum dragged me off into the garden.

She was rather formally dressed in a navy suit, but looked as lovely as ever. She didn't remind me of myself, I hadn't felt lovely in a while. In fact, my spirits had taken a definite downward turn ever since the meal with Chris Crozier, though I wasn't sure why anything she said should bother me.

Mum dusted the garden chairs off with a hanky and put her umbrella to one side. We sat opposite each other, a lacquered table between us.

'Why me?' I asked.

Smiling, Mum pushed carefully streaked hair from her eyes. Who did she remind me of lately? Sheila Hancock? Almost. Who was that actress turned MP? Glenda Jackson. Somewhere between the two.

'You're my only daughter,' she said. 'Who else would I choose?'

'It'll take some preparation,' I warned.

Mum laughed delightedly, the most genuine sound she'd made since our arrival.

'Like a virgin at the altar?'

'Margaret, please! Virgins, altars, I'd rather not dwell, thanks.'

She giggled again and as the rain spattered on the glass overhead we got reacquainted. It was something we had to do a lot. We'd always had to work at our relationship, and occasionally it was worth the effort. Persuaded and convinced to act the dutiful daughter, I agreed to be her bridesmaid as long as she had no say in what I wore. I knew Julia wouldn't need asking twice.

Arm in arm, a huge golf umbrella keeping off the worst of the rain, Mum showed me around the grounds.

At the back of the house a line of steep stone steps led to a flat roof. We walked up them together.

'I only discovered this a few weeks ago. I don't know

73

why Harry hadn't shown it me before. He knows I love a good view. I'll take you round the rest of the house when I get a minute.'

She folded the brolly before a gust of wind could take her sailing off the roof. I had visions of Mary Poppin...

'We could have waited for better weather,' I suggested loudly, as stinging rain caught me full in the face.

'That's the trouble,' Mum bellowed back. 'You can't guarantee what the weather's going to be like. Look.' She pointed westward.

The view *was* something else. Something worth getting wet over. Trees, again. Acres of them sturdily battling the inclement weather, their tops dramatically piercing the low-lying grey clouds. Fiercer sheets of rain, driven horizontal by the freshening winds and outlined against the occasional glimpse of sunshine, were heading our way.

I got my camera out of my bag, and positioned Mum in front of the spectacle.

'Don't smile,' I ordered, hoping for an atmospheric shot my lack of photographic talent was unlikely to capture. Knowing this Mum laughed anyway.

I had time for three quick snaps before the storm arrived and drove us back down the stairs.

Some poor sod in a butler's uniform stood at the entrance to the house clutching a brolly of his own, awaiting an arrival.

Our arrival, I realised as he opened the glossy black doors for our slightly dishevelled selves.

A double staircase swept upwards on either side of the wide expanse of hallway. Deep carpets, the colour a Cardinal with the top job just a death away would have found to his liking – were wool-rich, old but extremely well maintained.

Gleaming newel posts, tops rounded and smoothed by a century of hands and polish, reached elegantly towards the next floor and bedroom doors closed to curious eyes.

'Doesn't this do your head in?' I asked Mum quietly as we were relieved of our jackets.

'A little,' she admitted with a whisper. She led me to the dining room behind an oak door immediately to our right. 'It wasn't so bad when I was a visitor. I just felt a bit spoilt. Now I'm not sure how I'm expected to act,' she added.

I shook rain from my hair onto the carpet. The room was predictably wood panelled, ancient shotguns were suspended from the walls and fish, long since dead and gutted, hung in glass tanks. A pair of crossed broadswords gleamed on the wall opposite.

It should have been as dour as the outside of the building, but it was warm, inviting and, despite the fish and the guns, almost cozy. Even though it was June, a fire crackled in the hearth, taking the edge off the chill, and big, fat candles burned either side of the chimney breast.

The leaded window overlooking the gardens had a sill wide enough to seat half a dozen though its varnished surface held only family pictures in silver frames. I took a closer look. They were all photos, fairly recent ones too, of Mum and the Colonel and various members of his family. The Colonel hadn't changed in all the years I'd known him, though maybe his 'tache showed a little more grey and the receding hairline had receded all the way to the back of his head. They looked happy together, that was the main thing.

'Who are these people?' I asked, picking up one of the frames.

Mum peered over my shoulder. 'That's Harry's younger brother, Luke, you'll see him later. He's a lovely man, we get on really well. And that,' she added quietly, 'is Luke's daughter, Lorna. She's in prison, well, she *was* in prison. She's escaped.'

I gawped at her. She took a deep breath and rushed on. 'She got four years for being involved in an armed robbery. It's not common knowledge but the twelve million pounds or so that they stole has still not been recovered. Lorna's been in Styal for about two, maybe two and a half years. According to her father, with good behaviour she would have been out within the year. Lunacy.'

It didn't seem like lunacy to me. With all that money floating about somewhere, I'd have broken out of prison too. Even if it meant gnawing my way through the bars with my teeth. But didn't the family have enough dosh?

'It's been terrible for Luke,' Mum, the innocent, went on. 'He was a QC before he retired through ill-health. He has terrible arthritis,' she muttered, running a hand over her thick hair. 'They still don't know how Lorna got out. A bad lot, some of the Thompsons. One or two of the youngsters scare me half to death. It's been all over the news, though I don't suppose you've seen it. I know what you are like –'

'I did see it,' I interrupted, remembering the programme I'd watched with Mrs Buckham. 'I didn't realise one of them was a relative of Harry's, though. Why didn't you tell me before? I know about the rest of his wacky family, after all.' I glanced at her, hoping for an explanation. She played with a strand of her hair and shrugged, obviously upset.

'She's not likely to turn up here, is she?' I asked.

'God forbid!' Mum said and looked through the

window and shuddered. 'I half expect to see her walking over the hills. I wouldn't put it past her, though I imagine, at least I *hope*, the police have already thought of that possibility. They've been round here often enough with their questions.' Her mouth turned down at the corners. 'Lorna never liked me,' she added quietly. 'She hates the idea of any of this' – she gestured beyond the sprawling lands towards the horizon – 'going from the immediate family. It was bad enough when Harry's ex-wife walked out.'

I looked at her in surprise. She rarely mentioned Mary, the Colonel's former spouse, especially after she'd tried, and failed, to cite Mum during the divorce. 'Nobody was happy with the settlement *she* got. Luke's family thought she'd got too much, she thought she hadn't got enough, though it was sufficient for her to start her own business. It's pathetic, isn't it? It was supposed to be a marriage, not a financial free for all. It makes me so angry, this pettiness,' she spat.

As an expert in the trials, tribulations and pitfalls of inheritance and the like, I knew exactly what Mum was talking about. I could see why people left everything to cats' homes.

'I've never understood Lorna,' she continued. 'Luke gives – used to give – her an allowance, she was always his favourite, especially after the car accident. She was left partially deaf, you know. But he won't have anything to do with her at all now. He didn't go to the trial, won't even mention her name. This is the only picture of her, I wouldn't be surprised if he's burned the rest.' She paused to catch her breath. 'But I simply can't understand why she got involved. She had money, so why was she so desperate for more? Drugs, I shouldn't wonder. She wouldn't be the first in the family to indulge,' she added quietly. 'Please, Letitia, let's not talk about it,' she said, taking the framed picture and putting it back on the window sill.

The massive round dining table was nearly set for dinner. I could hear the clatter of cutlery being sorted from the kitchen that lay beyond another, smaller door.

Place names were already arranged and I glanced at them curiously as I edged around the table towards the fireplace. One leapt out at me.

'Chris F Crozier?' I stammered. 'What's she doing here?'

Mum, warming her backside by the fire, looked confused. 'Not she,' she declared. 'He. Chris Crozier's one of Harry's fishing cronies. That's where they are now, down at the lake. Why did you think Chris was a she?'

I didn't answer directly, still shocked at the coincidence. 'Is he from Texas?'

'Yes, do you know him?'

'No, but I think I know his daughter. She's the one turning George's farm into a health resort. I told you about it. Remember?'

Mum nodded and suddenly turned her back to me, so her front could get the benefit of the fire.

'Have you ever met her? I know she travels a lot. Maybe she's been here with her dad?' I had absolutely no idea why I asked Mum that, except a suddenly turned back always makes me suspicious.

'I don't think so,' she muttered into the chimney breast.

'Oh, you'd know if you had. Anyway, what's *he* like?' I asked, dreading a male version of his daughter. 'He's not religious, is he?'

'Religious? God no!' she exclaimed, as though I'd

suggested he was a child murderer. 'He's a pleasant enough man.' Her damp blue suit steamed quietly. 'I get the impression he wouldn't say boo to a goose. Or a salmon, come to that.' She sighed, took a deep breath and began, 'Though he is involved in –'

The door from the kitchen burst open, interrupting our conversation. Two women, furnished with piles of glasses, several decanters and a tray of silver cutlery entered the room.

'Coming though,' the youngest of the two bellowed.

Mum jumped back to allow them access.

'Hello, Margaret, get that suit off before you get pneumonia,' she commanded in a very un-Scottish accent. 'Doris, go and get the other plates, will you, chuck?'

Doris scuttled off.

The other woman turned to me and swept a short dark fringe off her forehead with the back of her hand. Honey-brown eyes, as shiny as wet paint, nailed me to the wall.

'So, you're the vegetarian daughter,' she declared.

I nodded, and she grinned, round and dampened pale cheeks pushing her eyes into narrow slits. In that five-second silence I learnt two things.

One, I wanted to rip the clothes from her luscious body and ravish her among the place settings. Two, I had a feeling she wouldn't mind.

I swallowed. I wanted a clear throat and an idea of what I would say before I opened my trap.

'Hiya,' I squeaked.

She stuck her hand out for me to shake. Her grip woke up a few tendons and every dozing hormone in my body.

'My God, Letty,' she said, her voice every bit as pleasing as the rest of her. 'You've got some bottle.'

'Have I?' I stammered.

'A veggy? In a place like this? I never cook anything that doesn't have a face. Sometimes I cook it with the face still attached.'

For the first time since vegetables had taken over my plate, I found I really didn't care. I would have cheerfully let her smear me in chicken soup, adorn me in avocado and prawn.

'I'm the chef, in case you hadn't guessed. Sarah Flowers, and I'm *very* pleased to meet you.'

What did she mean? Why the emphasis? And what a gorgeous name.

'Anyway, I must get back. That trout won't cook itself. And don't worry, I've got something extra special lined up for you. I wouldn't insult *your* palate with an omelette.' And with that she spun round and was gone.

Mum, hiding a smile, took me by the arm and led me upstairs. 'You won't remember her family,' she said.

'Whose?'

'Sarah's. They used to live near you years ago. There was a bit of bother and they moved to Manchester.' Mum rambled on.

'Margaret...'

She held up a finger. 'I thought Sarah deserved a second chance though. Christopher Crozier did too,' she added mysteriously.

'What are you *on* about?' I asked exasperated.

'I'm sure Sarah will tell you in her own good time.'

And with that the subject was closed.

We stopped outside a room on the first landing. Paintings hung either side, warlords in battledress staring down.

'Nice,' I observed. 'Very restful.'

'That'll be all, John, thank you,' Mum mumbled to the

butler waiting silently on guard by the bedroom door.

He bowed slightly, his pink balding scalp catching the light. He glided away without a word.

I just managed to hold onto my laughter until Julia answered Mum's knock. The minute I got through the door, I let rip.

'You don't mind sharing, do you? We've got so many guests this weekend it's a bit of a squash for everybody,' Mum asked.

Julia, bewildered, looked at me as I struggled for control. 'No, as long as she's not going to cackle hysterically all night.'

'I'll explain later,' I gulped. 'Margaret, haven't you got something to ask Julia?'

I went into the bathroom and left them to it.

Chapter 12

'So, what time's dinner then?' AnnaMaria asked.

'I dunno. When the gong goes I suppose,' I replied.

We'd all taken shelter in the room she shared with Mrs Buckham. Everyone except Julia felt overwhelmed by the furnishings, the building, the staff and the ornate trappings. I still couldn't get my mind off Sarah which, compared to Mum's intrigues, was a much more pleasant dilemma.

'Surely to God that's a male item of clothing,' AnnaMaria said, as Julia, finally dressed for dinner, reappeared from the bathroom. AnnaMaria fingered the heavy dark cloth of Julia's kilt, a surprise item she'd not mentioned before.

'Well, I'm not going to wear a sporran, if that's what you're worried about,' Julia declared. 'And knickers are a must.'

AnnaMaria laughed. 'And what clan is it? The Italian Black Watch?'

Julia peered down that haughty Roman nose and said, rather peculiarly, 'Read it and weep, darlin'. Read it and weep.'

★

'I thought she looked nice,' Mrs Buckham, who'd rediscovered the powers of speech, commented as Julia left the room. 'She carries it quite well. Not everyone can wear a kilt properly you know.' We watched in fascination as Sylvia applied her makeup. *The Masque of the Red Death*.

Or, in Sylvia Buckham's case, *The Masque of the Orange Death*.

AnnaMaria skittered across the bed. Already dressed for our first foray into posh pseudo-Scottish society, she decided to give Sylvia a helping hand. As a non-wearer, or very occasional wearer of slap herself, her advice to my old friend was 'less is best'.

I went back to *Coronation Street*, the only thing that could take my mind off a growling stomach and an intriguing cook.

'Finished,' AnnaMaria suddenly pronounced, and she spun Sylvia round on the dressing-table chair to face me.

'Gorgeous,' I said.

Mrs Buckham grinned.

Pale pink lips were complemented by a delicate dusting of blusher. Various greys and blues accentuated her broad-set eyes. AnnaMaria had even plucked some of the more unruly hairs from Sylvia's eyebrows.

'Are they loaded, this lot, then?' Sylvia enquired.

'Is it a husband you're after?' AnnaMaria asked mischievously.

'Not fussy,' the woman declared. 'Husband, wife, live-in lover. It's all the same to me. I'm too damned old to care.'

I tried to squash the picture that came vividly to mind. 'I thought you weren't interested in having a partner?' I asked.

'Letty, don't believe everything you hear. Especially if it's come from me. I'm sixty-two now, you know.'

Yeah, right. She was the only person I knew whose age went backwards. Even Mum was more honest.

'I wouldn't mind a bit of all this for myself.' She waved a nail-varnished finger around the room.

I could see her point. The paintings around the place, more ancient relatives, this time on horseback, were worth a bob or two. Mum had explained that the investment in sustainable forest was probably the best thing the Colonel's family could have done. There'd been no need to open the place to the public – hunting, shooting and fishing was the most they'd had to offer to the great unwashed. And, unlike the Grange, they didn't need to open it as a restaurant or a hotel.

Mrs Buckham blasted herself with Coco Chanel, or at least a very good copy of the famous French perfume. There was a loud BONG, from outside the room. Fire alarm, dinner announcement? BONG. Then a third and final BONG from somewhere in the depths of the house.

A soft tap on the door and Julia poked her head round. 'Ready?' she asked, grinning. 'You're just gonna love this!'

The three of us grappled for a last glance in the dressing-table mirror. Mrs Buckham had gone for the simple approach. Having saved her new suit for the following night's party she'd donned a blue waisted dress, probably the most conservative thing she now owned. AnnaMaria had settled for a long black skirt and a grey knitted silk top – definitely the most conservative thing I'd ever seen *her* in. Julia was in her kilt. My conventional trousers and jacket were nicely cut, if without an exceptional label. More importantly, I felt comfortable, if a little nervous.

84

I took a deep breath, then stepped from the bedroom onto the landing beyond.

We were like a trio of scared sheep with Julia, head collie, rounding us up. All I could see were half a dozen black-jacketed torsos heading into the dining room. From that quick glance I guessed they wouldn't be the sort to eat happily around the kitchen table, the telly blaring in the corner. Surprising what you can infer from a briefly glimpsed back view. Julia hurried us along. 'Your mother's already in there,' she whispered.

'Who are this lot, then?' I hissed back.

'His side, and their friends,' she answered. We edged further downstairs, the thick carpet and heavily flocked wallpaper absorbing any sound. 'There are only the four of us representing Margaret.'

'I know,' I replied quietly. 'She explained.'

'Will you two stop whispering?' AnnaMaria ordered loudly. 'Can't we just eat without all this song and dance? I'm starving. Sylvia, come on, these two are aggravating me to death.'

The two women brushed past us and headed into the dining room leaving me and Julia to scurry after them.

Chapter 13

'Don't you ever do that to me again,' AnnaMaria stormed as we headed from the dining room a few hours later.

The meal had been splendid, though Julia, currently the victim of AnnaMaria's animosity, had been the star turn. Mrs Buckham, suddenly overwhelmed by it all, had concentrated on her plate. All thoughts of potential partners were deported back into her world of fantasy.

The Colonel's family had a long male lineage. Apart from Mum, we were the only women present. Sadly, Sarah Flowers did not make an entrance, the food being dished up by the hard working Doris. And, as promised, I didn't get an omelette. Me and AnnaMaria, the only two veggies present, were presented with a kind of risotto stuffed with leeks and mushrooms, and a side dish of Parmesan wafers loaded onto a bed of roasted fennel. It could have come straight from the pages of the *Observer* Sunday supplement.

Maybe it did.

Everyone else got freshly caught trout, complete with face.

Conversation centred around either the following

day's engagement party or the fishing. For a family with a past, talk was disappointingly conventional. Skeletons obviously rattled around in private cupboards here. But, I reminded myself, we were strangers, moving in unfamiliar circles.

Our dinner-table companions were the older members of the Colonel's family. All had neutral, south of the border accents; I'd yet to hear a Scottish dialect. The younger, wilder elements (and especially those on the run from the police) had not been invited. However, I did get to meet and talk to Christopher Crozier. It appeared he had more than just a monetary interest in his daughter's latest project after all. We were dawdling over pudding, conversations quietly going on around the table, except for Julia who'd sunk the best part of two bottles of some posh dry white wine the Colonel had supplied from his cellar. Her chat to the Colonel's younger brother, Luke, who pointedly ignored Christopher all night, refusing even to refill his glass, had got louder and louder as the drink flowed. I'd had to concentrate hard on Christopher's words to drown out Julia's outrageous tales. The language was as ripe as the pear torte we were devouring. AnnaMaria's look had been thunderous as her name was bandied about. Mum, seated next to a very quiet and visibly nervous Colonel, was the perfect hostess and, trying to hold it all together, had simply ignored Julia. Always the easiest option.

My companion's accent was nowhere near as broad as his daughter's, the inflection softened, I learned, by international travel, though his enthusiasm for the new venture matched hers. He'd outlined his involvement as the cigars came out; Julia's Havana being bigger than anyone else's.

Christopher was a thickset man with wide shoulders

and a neck like a prop forward. He was balding, probably about sixty, and as uncomfortable in his hired suit as I would have been in a frock. He kept yanking at the collar that was rubbing his skin raw, as he talked. I imagined he'd be more at home in a big ten-gallon hat and jeans.

'I gave her the idea, you know,' he said in his laid back manner.

I smiled. 'Your daughter told me.'

He passed his cigar from one hand to the other, the tobacco crackling between his big fingers.

'Has she invited you to the opening yet? If she hasn't, then you can be my guest,' he drawled softly. Taking a drag on his cigar he squinted at me through the smoke.

'I've got my invite,' I said, remembering the unpleasant conversation I'd had with Amy. 'Her British rep came to see me.'

'Ah,' he said quietly. 'Amy.'

The name was loaded with messages left unspoken. I didn't pursue it.

'I was a bit curious about some of what your daughter was planning.'

'With the health farm?' he asked, surprised. 'I would have thought it was straightforward enough.'

'Well, maybe to you.' I defended myself. 'But the work's started already and AnnaMaria said it reminded her of a fortress.'

AnnaMaria, sitting opposite, looked up at the mention of her name.

Christopher laughed, head back, mouth open. 'Texas does that to a person. Bigger, louder, brasher, you've heard the clichés.'

I laughed quietly and said, 'But not you.'

He turned to stare at me appraisingly and then he

shrugged. 'I've been all over the world. Sometimes you need that brashness, sometimes you can leave it at home.'

'It just seems such a mixture,' I pressed on after a moment. 'Your daughter's business –'

'My business, I think you mean,' he interrupted. Not a ghost of a smile flickered across his face.

I cleared my throat. 'Okay, your business then. Contemplation on one hand, windsurfing on the other and then this face-lifting service she's got links with in Manchester.'

He frowned slightly, his heavily lined forehead pulling bushy eyebrows together. He glanced around the table. 'Fingers on the financial pulse, my family. I didn't start with much. Not every Texan has an oilfield to fall back on, you know.' He smiled suddenly. 'My first and most successful business, I should add, is for services supplied to State penitentiaries. It's a massive concern in my country, and yours too, I've discovered, though my involvement isn't something I'm particularly happy to advertise.' The frown exploded onto his face again. 'One mistake, one error of judgement and the press have a field day. Can't trust them. You tell them one thing and they print the opposite.' He growled and suddenly chomped down hard on his cigar. 'And anonymity can sometimes keep you commercially buoyant,' he added, pointing the soggy cigar butt at my face. 'I employ prison officers, catering services, transport, clean up crews. You've no idea of the size of these operations.' He paused, and I thought, but didn't quite dare put into words, that he should have offered his professional services to his host. Perhaps Harry's niece wouldn't be on the run if he had.

'Anyway, this surgery business. That definitely wasn't my idea. She's got a doctor friend, a plastic surgeon. Chris's premises will be an ideal place for her patients to convalesce. Do you disapprove too, Letty?' he asked, interested.

I thought for a minute, unnerved by his sudden mood swings and amazed that Mum hadn't sussed him out better. He'd slipped from jolly to angry to inquisitive in the time it took me to down another slurp of wine.

'I suppose I've got better things to spend my money on,' I said, finally.

Christopher chuckled, cheerful again. Brown eyes sparkled in the weathered folds of his skin. He scratched thoughtfully at a shaving nick on his chin and tentatively touched another one near his ear. He must have been shaving for the best part of fifty years. You'd think he'd have got it right by now.

'Let's talk about your mother,' he suggested. 'What do you think about her beau –?'

We'd gone on to discuss the couple. How Christopher had been introduced to the husband-to-be at some fishing championship at one of America's great lakes (don't ask me which one). And what the weather was likely to be like in Cyprus – the couple's chosen honeymoon spot – at Christmas. It turned out that Cyprus was the island where the Colonel had spent a lot of his Forces career. By this time it was late and soon guests started to head back to their rooms. The Colonel retreated, accompanied by Christopher Crozier. Luke followed, frosty, barely polite to the American guest as he tremblingly supported himself on two sticks.

Outstaying the rest, the women had been left alone. That's when the row had started. Julia was properly pissed by then and insistent that she'd said nothing out of turn.

'The fact that you were talking about me was enough. Haven't you got enough stories of your own without dragging me into it?' AnnaMaria snapped loudly.

'You're too sensitive, that's your trouble. When –'

'Julia,' Mum interrupted. 'Let's drop it, please.'

Mum turned to Mrs Buckham. She'd been nothing but pleasant to the overwhelmed shopkeeper and she'd expressed absolutely no surprise that she'd been chosen as my guest.

'Let me show you round the house,' Mum offered. 'Before we go to bed.' And she took her arm and led her from the dining room. 'I'll see you all tomorrow. Night everybody.' And the two women left the room.

We traipsed upstairs, AnnaMaria still chunnering at Julia's weaving figure.

It had been some years since I'd had to share a bed with Julia, and then I'd had some choice in the matter. But this fresh reminder of one of the reasons why our relationship had gone so horribly wrong was something I could have done without. Her snoring was bad enough but the elbows in the back were the final straw. Not to mention the grinding of teeth and quilt theft that she always denied. Selfish in life, selfish in bed, I'd once accused her before friendship had overcome that last bitter taste of a relationship turned sour.

Yet another poke in the back finally drove me out of bed.

'Julia, you're a pain,' I snapped at her comatose body. She snorted in her sleep by way of reply. The Colonel's house was one of the biggest I'd ever stayed in, you'd think he could have produced another bed from somewhere. I thought momentarily of AnnaMaria and Mrs Buckham, themselves in a similar position. How AnnaMaria would hate the very idea of sharing a bed with Sylvia, never mind the reality. But I was wrong about that. When I saw them after breakfast, the two women were evidently the most rested members of the household. Perhaps AnnaMaria had slept in the bath. I never asked.

Grabbing a dressing gown from behind the bathroom door, I headed downstairs. Perhaps a cup of tea, or a bottle of whisky would help me sleep.

Lights shone from under the dining-room door, even though my watch showed the time as almost three. I tapped lightly on the solid oak – the last thing I wanted to see was my mother in a smooch with the Colonel. About as much as she'd want to catch me in a smooch with some woman.

A voice called, 'Come in,' and I shoved the door open.

Sarah Flowers sat by the dying embers of the fire, a glass of Scotch in one hand and a neat, hand-rolled cigarette in the other.

She smiled and I was momentarily lost for words.

'Grab a pew,' she said and kicked a dining chair into position in front of the fire with a slippered foot. She wore an identical dressing gown to my own. I took the seat offered, declined the packet of Golden Virginia she waved at me, but accepted a tot of Glenmorangie, all without saying a word.

We sat in silence – a strangely comfortable silence – for a few minutes and then Sarah turned to me. She swirled the fiery golden liquid around in her glass and smiled. 'Do you know, you remind me of someone I went to school with.'

A response didn't seem necessary and the crackle of the fire filled the silence. I watched a spark gallop up the chimney.

'God,' she went on quietly. 'I used to have such a crush on her.'

I looked up, startled. That comment really *did* need a response.

Sarah laughed, a low sound starting at the back of her throat. 'Just testing,' she said before I could speak. I smiled at her mischievous face.

'So, where did you go to school then?' I asked her.

Sarah sucked her teeth for a second and leaned back in her chair to gaze at the ceiling. 'Pick a town,' she said and laughed. She took a sip of her whisky before she continued. 'I was born in Warrington. We moved to Manchester when Dad' – she paused – 'went away when I was four. We had a brief spell in Yorkshire, then back to Manchester and secondary school. I did a year at catering college learning my trade.' She took another sip and gazed at the fire. 'I dropped out of there, my own fault,' she added quietly. 'But I got my NVQs eventually, from the different institutions I worked at. I was abroad for a while, wandering through the States for a few months with an empty wallet. That's where I met Christopher Crozier, but I had to come home eventually.' She paused. 'I've had a pretty varied life really.' She let that sink in. 'And you? What's your story?' She glanced at me, her eyes, that rare colour, reflecting the glowing fire for just a second.

'I don't know where to start,' I said, pleased, if a little startled, at her candour. But I didn't really want to talk about me. I wanted to listen to that deeply pleasant voice, gaze at her honey eyes. I shook myself and let out a breath I'd been holding for too long.

Sarah looked at me curiously and got off her chair, picked up the bottle of Glenmorangie and shuffled over. A pair of pale blue shorts flashed under her dressing gown. She sat down cross-legged on the floor in front of me, muscular thighs making me catch my breath again.

She reached over to refresh my glass, resting her hand on my knee gently to balance herself. I was beginning to think I'd never breathe properly again.

'The beginning would be nice. Whatever you want to tell me, I'd love to hear.'

The Scotch and the conversation ensured I had at least a few hours' shut eye, despite Julia's poor bedroom manners.

It was only over breakfast; first up, best dressed *and best fed*, Dad used to say, that I was able to pore over what I'd learned. Sarah was gay, of course, first hurdle overcome at least, and I surmised that she was interested in me. Sometimes you can just *tell*.

I'd also found out that she had been working at the estate for the last couple of months. However, wanting to be near her mother, she was due at a new job that week, so Mum's big do was her culinary swan-song for the Colonel's household.

There were still mysteries surrounding her. Whatever favours and second chances Christopher Crozier had endowed on her, well, she wasn't telling me about them. She was frustrating and fascinating in equal measure.

I didn't really expect to see much of her that weekend, she'd be in the kitchens most of the time, but I felt the encounter had done me good. At worst, my libido had come back to life. At best, well, who knows? She'd taken my address with a wicked little smile and I'd made a note of her mobile number.

I would just have to wait and see.

Chapter 14

The party the following evening was one of the most raucous I'd ever attended, despite the fact that the average age of the attendees was about sixty-five. Drink flowed and the buffet, provided by Sarah Flowers, was cleared as though a bunch of marauding half-starved hostages had stormed through the place. Everyone danced to the sounds of pipe and drum, helped along by more than a few glasses of whisky. Mrs Buckham, not to be left out, dragged a few memories of Scottish country dancing from the cobwebs of her mind and twirled and reeled, using Julia and AnnaMaria who really *could* dance, as partners.

The great hall at the back of the house had a beautifully polished wooden floor, ideal for the sort of capers that were going on. Heavy velvet drapes covered the windows. I felt as though I'd stepped back a hundred years. I'd suffered Texan clichés lately, now I was getting the Scottish equivalent.

The Colonel, usually a commanding man, overcame nerves or whatever it was that had kept him silent until now, to make a short speech about his wife-to-be and present her with a delicate, yet obviously expensive, engagement ring. His family, her family (me), assorted guests and Sarah Flowers – escaping briefly from the kitchen with a trolley weighed down by an exquisite two-tiered-cake – toasted the happy couple.

I'd tried to have a conversation with Christopher Crozier, but bagpipes are not an easy instrument to talk over and we'd abandoned that idea for more spins around the room. I did catch his remark that he was looking forward to seeing me the following Friday at the opening of the health farm, but as far as conversation went, we had to leave it at that.

Fuelled by alcohol, I had absolutely no problem sleeping that night.

We planned to return home the following day and the morning was spent packing, nursing hangovers or, in my case, traipsing around the grounds for the last time with my mother.

The grass was damp from recent downpours but the sun was beginning to dry it out. A couple of swans and their offspring splashed at the far reaches of the lake. We stopped to look at the scenery and I broke the silence, clumsily but unintentionally spoiling a lovely moment.

'What is it with Luke and Christopher? Do they have some sort of history?'

I felt Mum stiffen slightly against my arm. 'What do you mean?' A sudden chill wind swept her hair from her face.

'I thought the swords were going to be whipped off the walls,' I blathered on. 'Not very fond of each other, are they?'

'I don't know,' Mum replied quietly. 'And to be honest, I don't want to know. I've got enough on my plate at the moment.'

I stopped and looked at her. I hated it when she was like this. 'Meaning?'

'Oh, that business with Luke's daughter worries me. I think...' she began. 'I've a feeling,' she corrected herself, 'that Lorna's been in touch.'

'Go on,' I said, trying to keep the alarm out of my voice.

Mum didn't appear to notice. 'With Harry. She's probably been after money, or help maybe, she was always close to him,' she went on in a rush. 'Please don't tell anyone else this, not AnnaMaria or Julia, promise?'

I nodded.

'It's just that he's been so secretive lately. And the phone' – she paused and scraped a tissue out of her pocket – 'I answered it one time. And this woman's voice' – she dabbed her nose – 'asked for him, Harry that is, before I had chance to speak. I asked who was calling and the line went quiet. Just breathing, you know? And she laughed too, which was worse, somehow.'

I waited for her to go on.

'It was Lorna, as sure as I'm standing here talking to you. She terrifies me.'

'Did you speak to her? Did you tell Harry?'

Mum shook her head. 'No. I hung up.'

'Tell the cops,' I said finally. 'Or change the number or tell Harry. Do *something*.'

'Telling you has made me feel better,' she said with a fleeting smile. 'But I do hope the police find her soon.' She looked at her feet and I wished I'd never brought the subject up.

'And you do still want to get married?' I asked bluntly.

'Yes, I do, of course I do,' she gabbled, a worried look on her face. 'I suppose Lorna being on the run scares me a bit and I'm afraid of losing my independence, too.

97

Does that sound silly? I just wish it could be different, that's all.'

How different did she want it to be? Despite the fugitive making silent phone calls, she'd stepped into the kind of life some people would kill for. The ring sparkling on the third finger of her left hand looked as though it could buy a small island in the tropics. Although I wasn't really worried that Mum might be in danger (I was sure Lorna had priorities other than jealousy at this point in her life), if I were in Mum's position I would have flogged the ring and bought the island.

A commotion in the lake stopped any further conversation. A rogue male swan splashed heavily into the water and the females, affronted by the new arrival, had set to with much squawking and flapping. It reminded me of my own brood at home and suddenly I wanted to be there, in the familiarity of my own backyard. It didn't even matter if the farm next door had been changed out of all recognition. I didn't care about the Thompsons or the Croziers, I just wanted to be home. I squeezed Mum's arm and, without another word, we set off back to the house.

Chapter 15

There's an old saying among the driving fraternity that the return journey is so much quicker than the outgoing one. Wrong. Surviving it at all was more a question of luck than judgement.

We'd not only swapped partners for the home run but cars too. My Land Rover, jittery on the drive down, would not start despite AnnaMaria's efforts and Julia, with a frosty smile, had begrudgingly strapped Mrs Buckham into the passenger seat of her sports car. Rather than wait for the AA to tow us home, the Colonel had generously agreed to have my Land Rover sorted out at the garage he used himself. So we were vehicle-less until Mum stepped in and offered her BMW.

'Are you sure?' I asked her, looking at the glistening, deeply tinted windows of her adored car. 'We could wait for the Land Rover to be repaired.'

'No need,' she said, kissing my cheek affectionately. 'I'll be heading home to Macclesfield next week sometime anyway. I'll come down in your Land Rover. We can do a swap then. I'm so glad we had a chat,' she added quietly. 'You've no idea how much better I feel.'

'Promise you'll ring me if you get another call, won't you?'

Mum smiled and nodded.

AnnaMaria, glad not to have to struggle with the peculiarities of the Land Rover's drive system, took the keys from Mum and shoved them in my hands with a happy grin.

'Ring me when you get home,' Mum said as she and the Colonel, quiet again, waved us off down the damp gravelled drive.

We caught another bunch of caravans heading back to England as we drifted up the slip road onto the motorway that would lead us home, and rather than stick behind the holidaymakers for mile after mile, I decided to indulge in a bit of lane dodging. But I was no match for Julia. She'd roared past us ages ago, and was probably already home with her feet up by now.

Once we'd passed the caravans, the newly tarmacked motorway wasn't too busy with only lorries thundering by in the middle lane.

Rain had begun to fall, not surprising, as we were heading for Yorkshire. Storm clouds were gathering high above us and it looked as though the steady drizzle was about to become a torrent. I already had the wipers going double quick, causing rivulets of water to run down the edges of the windscreen. The car got decidedly steamy. Each time a lorry passed, it splattered muddy water across the BMW and there were a couple more, taking advantage of the narrow slipstream the BMW offered, following maybe twenty yards behind. Too close for my comfort.

I kept the car going at around seventy, though the slightest pressure on the accelerator made the BMW roar forward – it felt like trying to control a Rottweiler. My tiredness, the weather and the sensitive engine combined to make motorway driving even more difficult than usual. I rolled my shoulders against the tension building in my muscles and tried to settle back against the upholstered seat.

'I'm going to pull off at the services,' I told AnnaMaria. 'I want to let this storm pass.'

She nodded. 'I could do with the toilet. Your mother should get this suspension seen to. It's too stiff. It does nothing for my bladder.' She stuck both hands between her thighs and crossed her ankles to prove her point.

The next services, the Scottish Widows Rest Area (unfortunate choice of name) was two turnoffs away. I glanced in the mirror in time to see one of the lorries edging into the slow lane, coming towards me on my left. I did what I'd done hundreds, probably thousands of times before and stuck the indicator on ready to turn in as soon as it was clear.

Nothing.

Great, problems with the electrics. I hoped Mum hadn't been skipping services on her car. If she had, I'd give her an earful when next I saw her, I decided.

I waited for the lorry on the inside lane to flash me over or pass. He did neither and all I could see through the side window as he narrowed the gap was the cab panel, rain-splashed matt red paint covering the faint outline of a company's name.

I put my foot down to give myself space and nudged the electric window open so I could use vaguely remembered hand signals.

AnnaMaria glanced at me curiously as wind and rain crashed into the cabin.

'Indicators are gone,' I yelled at her. She sighed.

I stuck my hand out and circled my arm furiously against the wind. The lorry, a flat-back carrying girders as far as I could see, picked up speed. We were in the same position again, doing slightly over seventy-five miles an hour.

'What *is* this dickhead doing?' AnnaMaria protested loudly and I glanced through the passenger window again. 'You'll have to slow down, let him pass on the inside,' she yelled.

My thoughts exactly. I took my foot off the accelerator, but we continued to gain speed. The noise from the road surface intensified and the wind howled and battered against the roof. What was this? I went for the brakes, but gently, refusing to panic. I had no idea how the car operated under stress. My foot went to the floor. I pumped steadily, a slight resistance and then the pedal was against carpet again.

'Letty?' AnnaMaria, bladder forgotten, turned to me, a nervous edge to her voice.

I couldn't answer, my jaw was clamped shut. I risked another look in the offside mirror. The lorry was still there. Some sensation, some *image* made me glimpse to my right and another lorry, articulated this time but with the same red paint and same anonymous cab, was suddenly on my shoulder, trapping me neatly in the middle lane. Where the hell had *he* come from?

I took a petrified look at the dash. Nearer eighty now. White lines flashed past my wheels. I concentrated on following the contours of the road as the speedometer edged upwards. It was climbing steadily towards ninety. The steering wheel began to shake.

The lorry to my right pulled slightly ahead and driving rain splashed up from his spinning tyres, streaking my windscreen. The wipers suddenly went dead. And my vision shrank from hundreds of feet to just yards ahead.

102

'Jesus, Letty,' AnnaMaria screeched above the racket.

I quickly jabbed the window control, at least they were still working. I was never quite sure why I did that, but the action probably saved my life.

I went for the brakes again as the articulated lorry, having pulled in front of me, thundered on. Through the downpour I caught a brief glimpse of the last neon sign for the service station, and still the brakes wouldn't respond.

They don't teach you how to deal with this during driving lessons, I thought manically.

'Letty, for fuck's sake,' AnnaMaria screamed as the flat-back to the left gained ground. The cab edged nearer to tower by the side of us. AnnaMaria, white faced, her mouth an 'O' of horror, scrambled away from her door. That move probably saved *her* life.

I jabbed at the barely responding brakes. The brake lights of the artic in front suddenly came on, its back doors growing frighteningly large, filling my rain-streaked windscreen. I could hear the steamy hiss of the air brakes.

I choked back a scream.

'Turn it off,' AnnaMaria shouted into my ear. 'The engine. TURN IT OFF!'

I shook my head. 'The steering lock, I can't, it'll jam!' I bellowed. I slammed down from top gear, missed the fourth, and somehow during a spiralling panic that I couldn't control any more, almost mashed the shift into reverse. Metal shrieked and the gearstick flew from my hand. There was a huge bang from under the bonnet. I could imagine engine pistons driven from their moorings and realised that Mum's BMW would never again get from nought to sixty in 9.5 seconds. Oh God, my mother's precious car! I took a hysterical moment to hope she was more fond of her daughter before going for the gears again. Our speed dropped from well over eighty to fifty within a heartbeat, and as the dashboard dials went beserk, another huge chunk of power was lost. The lorry immediately in front stroked his brakes in response. Steam and oil billowed from under the BMW's hood leaving greasy droplets across the smeared glass of the windscreen.

AnnaMaria clutched my arm fiercely. 'Brace yourself,' she screamed. Then she grabbed the handbrake and heaved.

A moment of utter silence before all four wheels locked and the smell of disintegrating rubber filled the cab. We spun, once, twice, narrowly missing the tail of the flat-back, and a nearside tyre blew as we went into a third and totally uncontrollable spin. I clung to the steering wheel, my fingernails instinctively sinking deep into the flesh of my palm, before another tyre blew and the sweat-lined leather was wrenched from my hands taking skin and a couple of nails with it. I felt the car leave the road and for one unbelievable second we were airborne. That strange moment of quiet returned before we bounced onto the hard shoulder. A vicious curtain of sparks thrown up from the wheel rims spattered against my side window. I was aware of AnnaMaria shrieking and her futile attempt to grab the spinning steering wheel. The vehicle, crunching and tearing itself apart with the impact, slewed broadside onto the incline of a grassy verge. We teetered for a moment and smashed sideways onto the motorway edge. The engine, wrecked and completely unresponsive, let out a final hiss of steam into the rainy air, and was silent.

'AnnaMaria?' I croaked. 'AnnaMaria, are you all right?' My companion was as quiet as the engine.

I dangled from my seatbelt and watched as cracks snaked across the oiled windscreen. It sounded as though a madman had been let loose in a bubble-wrap factory. A smell of petrol filled the cabin and I fought to unlock the seatbelt, refusing to think about the possibility of fire. My weight was against the belt and the lock itself had become mangled in the crash. I glanced at AnnaMaria who was slumped, dazed and shocked, against her door. The smell of fuel intensified. The windscreen, its pattern of smashed glass reaching from one side of the car to the other, suddenly collapsed inwards showering me in shards of glass. Wind howled through the gap and ahead of me I could see an empty motorway, nothing in either direction.

I tried the seatbelt again, panic making me clumsy and inept. I suddenly had ten thumbs, all of them scratched and bleeding. A single piece of windscreen fell onto my knee and I grabbed it and attacked the unyielding cloth of the seatbelt. I made a few bungled, then frenzied, attempts to cut through it – the glass slippy and unwieldy with blood – then the material tore apart and I fell onto AnnaMaria's lap. She groaned, a sound for which I was eternally grateful, and began to struggle against me.

'Letty, fuck, get off,' she mumbled and as she groggily looked around exclaimed, 'Petrol, I can smell petrol!' She whipped her seatbelt open in just a few short seconds, perhaps caught up with frantic memories of another fire she'd been the victim of years before. She suddenly shoved one hand under my backside and another on the back of my head and heaved me through the smashed windscreen.

I tumbled face down onto the verge and a handful of chewed up earth and oil-soaked grass found its way into my mouth. Coughing and spitting I staggered to my feet. I heard that first faint whoosh of fuel igniting and saw a blue and hazy ball of flame lick the cold damp air.

I turned to the BMW. AnnaMaria was half in and half out of the windscreen, struggling against the twin airbags that had finally been released. The back end of the car was beginning to burn; the smell of scorching carpets and luggage filling my nostrils. A piece of roofing material, blackened and flaming, was caught by a crosswind and fell onto AnnaMaria's back. I grabbed AnnaMaria's jumper and yanked her from the cab, rolling her over and over on the verge. Pain from my torn and bloody fingernails shrieked up my arms. AnnaMaria staggered to her feet, distressed and shaky.

'Come on,' I whispered and I reached for her hand. We shuffled away from the steadily burning vehicle, two yards, five yards, the heat of the fire warming my back, my knees grumbling at every step. There was a sudden hiss. 'Down,' I yelled, and I yanked AnnaMaria onto the grass verge as Mum's car was engulfed in one final roar of flames.

Chapter 16

'So you didn't get the number,' the young policewoman asked me gently for the third time.

I shook my head and the blanket fell away from my frozen and stiffening shoulders.

We were sat on the back step of an ambulance. AnnaMaria was inside, paramedics checking her for any injuries other than the superficial burns she'd got on the back of her neck. My hands were draped in white bandages that smelled faintly of antiseptic.

'You were very lucky,' the WPC insisted for the umpteenth time. 'There's not many walk away from an accident like this.' Her voice had a faint Scottish burr to it. We were only just over the border after all, the last three-hundred-yard skid having taken us from one country into another. 'And you say no one saw the incident? Apart from the lorry drivers, that is?'

I nodded, though 'incident' seemed a bit of an insipid word to use considering what had happened. I coughed, clearing the oily and grassy residue from my throat. The policewoman cautiously clapped me on the back.

'There was no one else on the motorway. We passed some caravans a while back . . .' And just as I said it the weekenders trundled by slowly rubbernecking as they passed the 'POLICE – ACCIDENT!' sign. 'Probably them now,' I informed her.

She was quickly on her radio and, through the drizzle that had taken over from the earlier downpour, I could see a uniformed officer waving the caravans over to the hard shoulder. I doubted they'd seen anything.

I shivered again, and watched as the fire chief checked the skeletal remains of the black BMW. I gazed at the smoking paint-stripped wreck and wondered, with more than a little irony, if it was a write-off. I'm dead, I thought as I imagined Mum's reaction. Home seemed so close and yet so very far away at this moment.

'Is there anyone you want to notify? Anyone waiting for you at home?' WPC something-or-other enquired. She brushed a piece of hair from the side of her mouth. I gave her Julia's mobile number. I would ring my mother with the news myself. She patted me on the back again and stepped away to speak into her walkie-talkie.

I looked over at AnnaMaria who managed a wan smile, despite the painful administrations of the paramedics. 'I want to go home,' she sighed. 'And I'm not going to the hospital. We'll be there all night.'

'But what about . . . ?' I interrupted, driven by years of conditioning. If you were injured in a car accident, then you had to go to hospital, they were the rules, surely?

'But nothing,' she said, agitatedly. 'You do what you like, but I'm going home to Liam. I'm not gonna die from a few blisters.'

I looked at my bandaged hands. I didn't suppose I'd die from a few scratches and missing nails either, though the pain intensified with every heartbeat. My tetanus jabs were up to date, the bleeding had stopped and my home called like a trumpet in the night, or an owl at dusk, or whatever the bloody saying was.

The policewoman came back eventually and handed me tea in a polystyrene cup. 'Courtesy of the service station manager,' she said with a smile. The wind caught her hair again and she stuffed it under her hat. 'We've contacted your friend ...' She flipped pages in her notebook, a sudden fierce breeze tried to take it from her hands and a spray of rain soaked the paper. 'Come on,' she said gently, hoisting me to my feet. 'Come and sit in the patrol car, it's warmer.'

Seconds later, still clutching the polystyrene cup, I was sitting in the back of the big orange-striped, two-litre Vauxhall.

'Your friend, Julia Rosco?'

'Rossi,' I corrected.

'Well, Miss Rossi was very concerned and she said she would organise a lift for you from the service station down the road. I understand your companion doesn't want to go to hospital. And I believe that's the same for you, is it?' she asked carefully.

I nodded my head in agreement. If AnnaMaria wasn't going, well, neither was I.

'We will need a statement from you both,' she said and went on to explain that the local police would pay a visit, or I could go to them. 'We will be pursuing this, Letty. If the car has been tampered with or if it's simply road rage or macho types proving a point, we will find out,' she emphasised. 'A car like yours very often brings out the worst in other road users.' She didn't add 'especially men', though I suspected that was in the back of her mind. 'And with a bit of luck some of the incident will have been caught on the motorway cameras.'

'Oh God! My terrible driving caught on *Police! Action! Stop!*'

The policewoman smiled again and I realised just how young she was. She was even younger than AnnaMaria, and even more self-assured.

'We're going to take your vehicle to the pound in Carlisle. Checks will have to be done on it, you do realise?'

I grunted a yes and remembered the sudden failure of the electrics and brakes just before the crash. Maybe it had been Mum's fault all along, maybe she should have had it checked over more often. Or maybe . . . ? But no, the idea of sabotage was too ridiculous to contemplate. Unroadworthiness, some fault or other was the most likely cause. The arseholes in the lorries simply made a bad situation worse.

The policewoman looked at me with concern. 'Are you sure you don't want to go to the hospital? Shock can be a very nasty thing.'

I shook my head. Eventually, after a few more questions, during which the police had waved on the holidaymakers (as I'd suspected, no help there), organised the removal of the BMW and conducted a sweep up operation around the glass-covered hard shoulder, the young WPC drove me and AnnaMaria to the nearby Scottish Widows Rest Area. She left us there, refugees from an incident we were lucky to walk away from.

'Jesus, Mary and all the frigging Saints,' Julia declared as she drove us home. She'd collected us within a few hours of our being deposited at the services. 'I always knew that frigging car was a death trap,' she raged, though I'd never heard her say *that* before. Concern had driven her into an angry frenzy. Where tea and sympathy might have turned me into a quivering wreck, loud words and much swearing kept me sane.

AnnaMaria ignored her and instead wistfully stroked the speckled grey interior of the Suzuki Vitara Julia had chosen to collect us in. Now would have been an apt time to inform the young woman that the vehicle was legally hers, though she would have dragged Julia forcibly out of the driving seat if I had. That little bit of good news would have to keep.

'We'll have to see,' I mumbled, reluctant to share what I already knew and even more reluctant to put into words my suspicions. 'The police are doing checks.'

'And those lorries? What about them?' Julia demanded.

I shrugged. I'd already explained about the cameras, I didn't feel I needed to repeat it all again. And I was determined to keep my own stupid but niggling worries to myself.

'And all that luggage, gone,' Julia went on, trying to look at me and the road at the same time. 'All your clothes and Sylvia's best suit, she'll pitch a fit.'

'Just drive, Julia,' AnnaMaria suggested tiredly and after another half-hearted tirade, she did just that.

Chapter 17

Calderton welcomed us home with its usual indifference. As we drove through the village we passed two trucks on the Halifax Road. AID CONVOY in large white letters was etched across the black panels. I was too tired after the long and tedious journey and too wired after the horrendous crash to wonder or, sadly, even care how the collections were going. But finally I managed to put to the back of my mind our lucky escape.

My home was how I'd left it, but next door was turning into Calderton's very own Hollywood.

Julia, who'd spent the last hours staring fixedly through the windscreen, finally broke her silence.

'Home, at last,' she exclaimed as she drove into my yard.

I looked through the window and shock coursed through my body again. Stan was waiting for us and he turned to wave from his precarious position on top of an upturned wooden crate. He'd obviously been getting a good eyeful over the fence. He jumped down to greet us.

'Are you all right?' he yelled as I crawled out of the Suzuki.

Stiffening muscles screeched in protest as I stretched my arms and tested my aching legs. My fingers stung under the tight padding of bandages.

Stan shuffled over in his strange sideways gait.

'I'm okay,' I informed him.

'Well, you look bloody terrible. Lunatics on the roads nowadays. Lorry drivers! Can't trust 'em, can't shoot 'em.'

Mrs Buckham came hurtling out of my front door.

'I wanted to come along but she wouldn't let me,' she said and glared at Julia. 'The kettle's on, I've run a bath, just needs topping up. Oh, look at your poor hands,' she said, and began to wring her own. She turned to AnnaMaria. 'I've told June and Andy. They said they'll bring Liam over when you're ready. Dreadful, dreadful,' she wailed. 'I slept all the way home. Didn't see a thing.' And with that she grabbed AnnaMaria by the shoulders and led her into the house, fussing and tutting all the while.

'Just come and 'ave a look at this before you go in,' Stan ordered. He took a crumpled handkerchief from the sleeve of his holey home-made jumper. An odd place to keep it for an adult, especially a man, I thought idly. He honked a good one into the cotton, had a quick peek to make sure he'd not blown his brains out, and waved me after him.

I followed him with a sigh, as disinterested as I was ever likely to be at the neighbourhood alterations, that is, until I saw them. Stan scrambled the hundred yards or so back to the wooden crate. 'It won't take us both,' he observed and placed a rough and ready hand under my arm to hoist me onto the box. 'Mind yer bandages, though.'

I propped myself against the fence, steadying myself

with my elbows. The barrier was smooth and smelled of new wood and yacht varnish that had only just dried. Other smells drifted over, smells I would never have associated with George's farm.

Pot-pourri and wood shavings, fresh grass and mint, a piney smell, similar to the forest we'd driven through in Scotland, and something that reminded me, strangely, of the local baths. I reached up to the top of the fence, being careful not to bang my hands, and stretched onto tiptoe for a look.

Walt Disney would have been proud. There was freshly unrolled lawn as far as I could see. Neat borders of newly planted flowers and herbs lined the grassed areas, interspersed with half-grown miniature trees every ten feet or so. A man with an electric roller was carefully flattening the velvety grass. Trendy decking painted in cool mint and sunblaze yellow had been built on either side of the front door. Plastic awnings over the wooden planking slapped lazily in the light breeze.

The driveway was covered in virginal multicoloured stone chippings and had been designed to skirt a half circle in front of the house (no longer could it be classed as a *barn*). I could see that the double doors were propped open and as the breeze freshened I got a whiff of gloss paint and new carpets.

'Good God,' I muttered as a hand pulled at my sleeve. Though I knew the previous few weeks had been spent redesigning the innards of the old place, I was still amazed what a difference a few days' painting and laying stone chippings could make.

'Let me get a proper look,' Julia hissed. 'I didn't get a chance before the cops called.' I clambered down as Stan helped Julia take my place.

'Day and night, they've been working. All Yanks as

well, an army of 'em and not a local lad in sight. All this has taken them no time at all,' Stan marvelled in hushed tones. 'Not unionised though, I bet. Hope they got well paid.'

I looked around at my more familiar property. 'Stan, where are the hens?'

'I left 'em locked up,' he explained, turning to me. 'What with all the noise there's been and the bloody arc lights, it's been like Blackpool Illuminations around here. The damned birds didn't know whether to sleep or lay eggs. Pandemonium.' He shook his head.

Stan searched through his overall pockets and dragged out my spare keys. 'Everything is spick and span and you can get a great view from the bedroom window, if you've a mind.' He coloured slightly as he realised what he'd said.

'Thanks, Stan,' I said, tiredly ignoring the implication. 'Sylvia will have the kettle on I imagine. Do you want a cuppa?'

'No, no. The sheep,' he said making peculiar shearing motions with his hands.

He took off down the drive towards his van, but turned towards me again. 'If there's anything I can do, you know where you can find me. You can't work with your hands in that state, after all.' He shuffled down the yard towards his old truck, waved a last cheery farewell and was gone.

I took a few painful minutes to release the chickens from their hen houses. Some remained prostrate and dozy on their nests, others came screeching out as though it were VE Day. I had a quick look in the garage before I went indoors to face Sylvia's questions. I didn't bother trying to open the door to the Suzuki parked in there, my fingers complained at the very thought, so a quick inspection confirmed the appraisal I'd given the vehicle on the unpleasant drive home. Andy had done a wonderful job. Though the paintwork was now splashed with muddy rain, the jeep looked a lot newer than its five-year-old registration plates indicated. A thought occurred. I hoped Mum's mechanics were as thorough as Andy, who'd learned a lot of his skills alongside AnnaMaria. His work may have been slow, but he was meticulous when it came to engines. His ex-partner was the same. Mum wouldn't leave such things to chance, would she? The alternatives that floated through my mind were becoming more ridiculous the more distance I put between myself and the crash. I realised that I'd have to wait a while – for the police report – before I'd know anything definite, as frustrating as that might be.

I wasn't entirely sure how I'd present the jeep to AnnaMaria without a load of hoo-ha, but that was something I didn't need to worry about. She accepted it with a few tears and extremely good grace the following morning. I was relieved I didn't have to beg her to take it off my hands.

A pile of post and the surprisingly uncompromising figure of Mrs Buckham awaited me as I finally stepped over the threshold. 'Ring your mother,' she ordered. 'And then eat.'

An invalid's portion of soup was placed on the table with a farmer's ration of thick, unevenly sliced white bread. My companions were dutifully eating their own share of the feast.

Even AnnaMaria, craving Liam, her bed and twelve uninterrupted dream-free hours of sleep, was doing as the older woman demanded.

I went to the hall phone to ring Mum. She managed

116

to jump to the same conclusions I'd just dismissed. But half an hour of me playing down the facts did the trick and she was finally about convinced that the accident had been just that. With 'All right, I'll come over on Friday,' and 'I don't care about the damned car,' still rattling the lines between Scotland and Calderton, I hung up.

Eventually, balancing a spoon between two bandaged fingers and weak from exhaustion, I ate my bread and soup.

Chapter 18

The previous night Julia had made an offer of help. I'd given her two choices. See to the farm or see to Liam. As Mrs Buckham had opted to take Liam to playschool, Julia, God save us all, was left with the chickens. If I'd had the energy I would have followed her around with a camcorder, none of her friends would have believed it otherwise. I could hear the shrieking and cursing from my bedroom. The clatter of buckets and the hissing of water exploding from a hosepipe opened too fiercely filled the early hours of the morning.

'Shit! Fuck! SHIT!' Julia bellowed. Translated, that meant 'Get up bitch, I can't *do* this!'

I got out of bed. If I couldn't record the moment at least I could watch it.

Julia stood in the middle of the yard. Hens – blarting, squawking and flapping around in a drenched kind of terror – surrounded her. She was clutching the hosepipe, desperately trying to turn it off. She was as soaked as the panicking hens, right to the skin, and several crates of smashed eggs lay at her feet.

She'd been doing her gentleman-farmer bit. She wore neither wellies, nor decent waterproofs. She wasn't even wearing jeans, just natty blue pants, a cream blouse with the sleeves rolled neatly above her wrists and, get this, *suede* ankle boots. I don't know whether she expected the hens to eat politely from her hands and obligingly lift their rear ends to enable her to get at the eggs, but we'd been down this road years before. She'd obviously forgotten about ungrateful animalistic behaviour.

She suddenly looked up at my window and with a malevolent grin turned the hosepipe on me. I stepped back, sucking in breath as I anticipated an icy blast but, fortunately, the windows were shut and water merely splashed against glass. I managed a stiff two-fingered salute at the sodden figure of my oldest and most loyal friend.

'I'll come down,' I yelled.

'Ooh,' Mrs Buckham greeted me as I ventured downstairs. She had a letter in one hand and a boisterous, neatly dressed Liam in the other. 'Ooh,' she said again, louder this time. 'It's done.'

'What is?' I asked as I carefully unwound my bandages. I'd abandoned the idea of a wash for the moment as I wanted to assess the damage to see when I could get back to work. I obviously couldn't leave it to Julia for long.

'The shop. The gas is reconnected and my refit is just about complete. At long last. And I've had this wonderful idea,' she enthused, though it was a while before I found out what that idea was.

'I've been meaning to talk to you about that,' I informed her as the last of the bandages peeled away. My stomach lurched at the slightly grisly sight. 'I met Liz a while ago.'

'Who?' Sylvia asked.

'Liz. One of the people working on your shop. Red hair, smashed in face.'

Mrs Buckham looked at me curiously as Liam began to squirm. 'Come on!' he said loudly. Mrs Buckham's grip got stronger. Liam stopped wriggling.

'Liz? Liz? Don't know any Liz. Red hair, smashed in face you say?' She shook her head, puzzled. 'Frankie Field was supposed to be doing it. You know Frankie. Used to work at the abattoir. He's marvellous with wood. Put my floor in last time. Built like a brick wall, hands like shovels...'

'Yes, I know Frankie. But this was definitely a Liz. No doubt about it. Said she'd come to help out.'

Mrs Buckham shrugged. 'Perhaps he hired one of the clan. He's got relatives all over the place,' she said dismissively. 'Anyway, it's finished, I don't care who's done it. I've not even had a look yet. It'll be just like *Changing Rooms* when I get there. I bet I end up in tears,' she said, laughing to herself, as she pushed Liam out of the door.

I discovered that my hands were better off without their wrappings. I replaced the bandages with heavy plaster, carefully flexed my stiff digits and slightly stiffening back, and ventured outside.

Julia had finished her chores and was sweeping up the remains of today's ruined eggs.

'Don't ever ask me to do this again. Ever,' she groaned. 'Look at the state I'm in, and does anybody care? No.'

'Julia,' I said, smiling. 'Your angel's wings are surely being knitted as we speak.'

She sniffed, readily convinced of her own saintliness. 'Come and look at next door's, you won't believe what's arrived now.'

She abandoned the hosepipe and waved me over to a pair of stepladders leaning against the fence. Using my elbows for balance, and gritting my teeth against the pain, I peered over.

Horses, three of them, in the field beyond the newly picketed garden. A stable on wheels had been delivered during the night and several cars and a blue van were parked by the front of the house. A board at the end of the driveway proclaimed:

EAST BROOK HEALTH CLUB
CFC Inspirational Health and Beauty Inc. Prop. Chris F Crozier.
NOW OPEN FOR BOOKINGS

Suddenly a figure carrying a large cardboard box shuffled out of the house. The woman, dark hair tumbling around her face, staggered over to the van and dropped the box on the floor. She looked back towards the house with a frown and then reached up to open the back of the vehicle.

'Christ,' I said as my stomach suddenly did a handstand. 'Sarah Flowers!' I forgot my backache and smarting fingers.

Perhaps the wind had carried my words, or perhaps she just sensed someone's presence. Either way, Sarah looked round and spotted me gawping over the fence.

'Hello,' she said. Her smile was somewhere between smug and triumphant.

'Hiya,' I said, grinning stupidly. 'What are *you* doing here?'

'Working. I told you about my new job, remember?' She rested her fists on her hips. 'Just thought I'd keep the location a surprise.'

'Shock, more like,' I muttered, the smile still stretched across my face.

121

'Why don't you come over? I'll show you round the place.'

'Is Chris there?'

I felt a poke in the back of my leg.

'Who are you talking to?' Julia demanded.

'If you mean Christine, she's somewhere with Amy, I think,' Sarah said, glancing towards the horses. 'I've not seen her for hours though. Come on, I'll make you a coffee.' And she beckoned me with a flick of her head. My innards melted.

'No Julia, you're not.' My words were final.

'Oh, Letty. I won't cramp your style.'

'Which part of "no" don't you understand?' I wasn't going to win any marks for using this particularly unoriginal comment, but it worked with Julia. She stopped trying to persuade me to invite her next door and instead resorted to sulks and some muttered comments about 'stalking'.

'Look, I'll be an hour, an hour and a half tops. Okay?' I insisted.

I left the house alone, having changed into chinos, my favourite creamy cotton jumper, and having bound fresh plasters around my finger ends.

In fitter days I would have climbed over the fence but today I had to haul my carcass down my yard, along the road a spell and up the sprawling magenta and baby blue gravelled driveway that now led to East Brook Farm.

The sun came out, the wind dropped and a fantasy (plus coffee) waited for me.

'Your mum told me a bit about the accident before I left Scotland. You must have been terrified,' Sarah said when she heard my tale of disaster.

122

I nodded and carefully put my coffee mug back on the kitchen table. 'I've had some horrible moments in my life, but this was probably the worst.'

'Horrible moments, eh?' she asked with a grin. 'You must tell me all about them someday.'

Sarah was wearing her chef's suit: blue striped pants and crossover short white jacket. Her head was hatless though I'd noticed a stripy skull-cap hanging on the back of the kitchen door.

The huge whitewashed room sported stainless-steel fittings and stripped elm, and with a work surface running down the centre of the room, the kitchen screamed 'new'. Knives and steel containers, not yet used, hung from hooks screwed into beams criss-crossing the ceiling.

'This must have cost a packet,' I ventured.

'I know. Fab, isn't it? I've worked in a few kitchens, hell-holes some of them, but this is the first one I've ever had a say in. Look at all this stuff.' And she opened drawers and cupboards full of equipment. 'I'll probably never use half of it. A health farm? I can't imagine preparing much more than carrot soup and fancy salads, can you?'

She took a couple of hefty Sabatier knives from the hooks and began juggling them, an occupation that had obviously become popular in Calderton. My heart leaped to my mouth, a place where it had almost taken up permanent residency. I suddenly realised Sarah was trying to impress me and that pleased me in some juvenile part of my brain.

She put the knives away just as the kitchen door swung open.

'Sarah, honey, can you make lunch for six today? Letty, darlin', great to see you again,' Christine Crozier

123

bellowed when she saw me. 'Lord, whatever happened to your hands? You haven't been tryin' to teach her to juggle, have you, Sarah?' She laughed.

'A car accident,' I explained, warily taking in the spirited figure of my new neighbour. She was dressed in a royal blue jogging suit, mud spattered and smelling of horse manure.

'Ouch,' she said sympathetically and went to the sink to wash her hands. 'Sarah, make that seven for lunch. You can be persuaded to stay, can't you, Letty? We eat about two. Sarah here can cook up some fine vegetarian fodder I've heard.'

Sarah grinned at me. 'Your wish is my desire,' she declared.

My heart left my chest again but, unfortunately, I had to refuse. I shook my head; I didn't trust my mouth.

'Well, never mind, another time. And what do you think of the place?' Chris asked. Her healthily rosy cheeks were splashed with what I hoped was only mud.

'It's coming along,' I managed.

Chris exploded with laughter. 'Oh, you British,' she said with a shake of her head and still chuckling, she marched out of the door.

'She likes you,' Sarah declared, donning her hat.

'Oh, she wouldn't if she knew,' I replied, curiously watching an expert getting to work.

'Knew what?' Sarah asked in surprise, pausing as she retrieved salad from an enormous steel fridge.

'That I'm gay.'

'Where the hell did you get that idea from?' she asked in the blunt tone that was just beginning to seem familiar. 'She knows I am, hasn't stopped me.'

'But she's religious, isn't she? Amy said –

'Christ, don't listen to *her*,' Sarah interrupted, turning

124

to the work surface. 'I won't even let that bitch into the kitchen.' And she crashed a knife into the guts of an innocent iceberg lettuce.

I jumped as the metal connected with the wooden chopping board.

'Do you know, Chris's dad recommended me for this post. I think your mum might have put in a good word too. She used to know my family, from years back,' she added. 'I've been feeding the pair of them for weeks on and off at the Colonel's place in Scotland. He knew I wanted to get back to England. Funny, isn't it, how these coincidences work out? And with you being next door.' She grinned and let the rest of the sentence slide. 'Anyway, Amy...' She began to slice onions with an expertise I'd only ever seen on the telly. 'Amy is a toadying, belly-aching piece of shit. And you can quote me.' She scraped the onions into a dish and began to mix a salad dressing. Olive oil, garlic, lemon juice and a variety of herbs. She shoved half a dozen tomatoes onto a long metal prong and held them over a savage heat on the gas hob built into the work unit. Switching it off, she set about freeing them of their skins. 'Skinned tomatoes are gorgeous in salads, did you know?'

I shook my head.

'Amy tried her damnedest to keep me out of this place. I still don't know why. She told Chris I was gay, thinking that would do it.' Sarah laughed at a memory. 'Guess what Chris said. "Hell, honey, she's here to cook, not fuck."'

My mouth dropped open.

'That's the exact same expression I had when Chris told me. Religious? It's the sort of religion I could handle to be honest.'

'But all those prayers, all that "Lord Save Us" stuff. I

was beginning to think this place was going to be some sort of cult headquarters,' I said, admitting to a fear that I'd only ever shared with Julia. I went on to explain our afternoon out at the Grange, including the part when Amy had gripped my arm in warning. Sarah laughed at my concerns, showing slightly crooked eye-teeth, an imperfection that was somehow enchanting. She added her own thoughts on the subject. 'Chris is from the heart of the Bible Belt. I suppose it leaves its mark. Have you ever been there. Texas?'

'Not Texas, no. San Francisco to see my uncle. Now *that* was amazing.'

And at that point the subject of Chris and Amy was dropped and holiday stories were exchanged instead. A much happier and infinitely less complicated conversation followed.

My hour was suddenly up and I had to get back before Julia was tempted to torch the farm to get my attention. Sarah's lunch for six was ready. An extra large chicken had been smeared in herbs, butter and garlic and was frazzling in the oven. The salads and cold summer soup she'd prepared were chilling in the fridge. I got up to leave and pain as fierce as a kick in the kidneys shot across my back and down my right leg.

'Jesus!' I exploded, clutching the chair for support.

Sarah came over to me, concern on her face. 'What? What's up?'

'My back, I twisted it in the crash.' I sat down again with a thud.

Sarah leaned over me. 'You seen a doctor?'

'Just the medic in the ambulance. It's whiplash. I've got painkillers at home.'

'Oh, you don't need those,' she said, and smiled. 'Come on, let me help you up, I know just the thing.'

126

'I've got to get back,' I began.

'Come on. Give me half an hour, I'll have you dancing out of here.'

Firm, long-fingered hands helped me to my feet and I gave myself up to her. I didn't need a lot of persuading.

She led me to a newly glossed door. The pain as I straightened up became almost manageable.

'My room's down here, in the basement,' she said. Whitewashed walls towered over old and well-worn stone steps. Sarah led the way, wiping her hands on a tea towel tucked into the waistband of her apron. 'Okay?' she asked with a smile.

I nodded, suddenly bashful. Here I was, willingly, unquestioningly, following a woman I didn't really know into the privacy of her room. God knows what I was expecting. I hoped she wasn't expecting too much from me, I thought as my bludgeoned fingers clutched tentatively at the stair rail.

Her room was similarly whitewashed, warm and brightly cheerful. A high single bed was tucked in a corner with an Indian throw in yellow and red tossed over it. A few boxes, as yet unpacked, were stacked to on side. Framed pictures, originals in oil of country scenes, on the walls. I recognised the view of the Colonel's place in Scotland and another that had clearly been painted from the flat roof I'd visited with Mum. I wondered for a moment if Sarah had painted them herself.

One of a woman, naked, half turned away from the artist, was painted in a style very different to the others. And there was something very bold about the portrait, too. As though the sitter had an intimate knowledge of the person wielding the paint. Still, what did I know? A Turner prize judge I ain't.

Only the top two panes of the window were above

ground level, and the light from these fell directly onto a thick, room-sized rug. Sarah switched on a lamp and any gloom retreated to the corners.

'Do you know what these hands are good for?' she asked, grinning again.

'Apart from slicing onions?' I replied. 'Or juggling?' Suddenly, I felt giddy.

'Massage,' she stated.

I was vaguely disappointed.

'Get on the bed,' she ordered. 'Keep your top on if you like, but flesh is best.'

I risked a glance at her to see her expression but she was already turned away from me, fiddling with bottles on an old colour-washed dresser. I pulled my T-shirt off; I didn't need telling twice. One way or another, this woman was going to get her hands on me and, as far as I was concerned, this was a fine way to start.

Chapter 19

I didn't quite dance out of the place, but Sarah's kneading and stroking, manipulations and hot, hot hands got me straightened up and as breathless as I'd ever been in my life.

Finally, she saw me to the door.

'Perhaps you'll be able to stay longer at the launch.'

'I hope so,' I agreed. 'Though you'll have a busy day of it, won't you?'

Sarah ran a hand across her forehead and I got a delicate waft of the oil she'd used on my back. Strands of dark hair clung to her round and healthy cheeks. 'It's all in the preparation,' she declared, smiling. 'Like most things.'

She reached for my arm and rubbed it gently. 'See you soon, then.' And she leaned forward to kiss me on the side of my mouth. I don't know whether Sarah's timing was poor or if our luck was out but as her lips found my cheek Amy appeared in the doorway.

'Oh, don't mind me,' she muttered as she snuck past. 'And before you try and throw me out, Sarah, your employer asked me to get the fruit juice. You've no objections, have you?'

A slow flush of anger rose in Sarah's cheeks. 'Help yourself to the lemons,' she suggested to Amy's back. 'They should suit.'

Amy glanced over her shoulder. She gazed at me, expressionless, and followed it with a look towards Sarah that would have turned a lesser woman into a quivering, shivering wreck.

Of course, with every fantasy there had to be a downside and two individuals that I'd not particularly wanted to bump into again accosted me as I headed away from the multicoloured driveway.

'I've not got a flat tyre that needs fixing,' I said as I edged past Gaz and Darren. The two boys leaned on the gatepost trying to look cool and menacing. But twenty-first-century *Boyz 'N' the Hood* they were not.

'Somethin' a bit worse, we heard,' Gaz offered.

Obviously Mrs Buckham hadn't even made it to the bus stop before she'd started blabbing.

'Yeah, well, shit happens,' I said.

Darren made a weird croaking sound that I assumed was a laugh. He was of the age where a boy's voice runs up and down the octaves, not quite managing to settle on any one in particular.

They grabbed their skateboards and shuffled after me when they realised I wasn't going to stop and chat.

'Was it bad?' Gaz asked.

'Were you smashed up much?' Darren interrupted his skinny partner. He ran his fingers through his disgustingly healthy hair.

'Walking wounded,' I replied and waved my battered hands at them.

'Nasty,' Darren pronounced.

'Could have been worse,' Gaz decided.

'Could have been dead,' Darren acknowledged, sagely.

We trudged in silence for a minute.

I stopped. 'Did you want something?'

Gaz took a breath. 'We've got some information.'

'On?'

'On what?' Darren looked puzzled.

'You've got some information on...?'

'Oh. That tyre place on Halifax Road.'

I continued to walk. 'What about it?'

Gaz hurried ahead and began to walk backwards to make sure he'd got my attention. He glanced at Darren slyly.

'I've no money,' I said, recognising the look.

'Aah, come on. Just a couple of quid.'

I searched in my pockets; it was probably the easiest way to get rid of them. 'A pound and some change. Take it or leave it,' I opened my palm towards Gaz. The money was whisked from my hand and into a deep jeans pocket before I could react.

He dropped his skateboard to the floor. 'It's s'posed to be an Aid Convoy, right?'

'Right,' I said cautiously.

'Have you seen those vans? Not like any convoy I've ever seen on telly. Brand-new Mercedes fer Christ's sake. And if that bloke running it is doing Aid Convoys then I'm a...' He thought about his punchline for a minute.

Darren beat him to it. 'A lesbian!' he said and howled with laughter.

Gaz didn't even grin and sullenly stalked off. 'You've got to think of better ones than that, y'know,' he said as Darren hurried after him.

'Well, you couldn't think of one at all...' I heard his friend say as they left me at the farm gates. I shook my

131

head. I'd just lost a couple of quid to a pair of aliens. Talk about men are from Mars.

I escaped back home, stomach rumbling, back no longer aching, emotions in a tizz, to find Sylvia packing what remained of her clothes left from the BMW. She'd not said a thing about her suit, though the word insurance had already been mentioned a couple of times. I made a mental note to arrange its replacement. It was the least I could do.

Her niece, Janice, was in the kitchen with her. Janice was a reporter for the *Calderton Echo*. AnnaMaria hated her with a vehemence I neither understood, shared nor could do anything about. 'Fucking ambulance chasers,' was the only thing she would say about Janice and the hacks she shared her working life with.

They ignored each other as much as possible.

'AnnaMaria's gone out,' Mrs Buckham informed me. 'I told her not to, with the accident and everything, but she's gone to the garage. That Amy's just been on the phone to ask her to look at that car she bought. AnnaMaria said it would take her mind off things.'

It would take her mind off wanting to shove Janice's head down the toilet at least.

'And I'm going too,' Julia piped up. 'Much as I'd love to do another stint of chicken sitting, the world of automobiles awaits. I'd better find out what Amy's griping about. I don't want her on my case.' And Julia, dry and dressed, gave my hands the once over, made a whispered comment about 'my latest squeeze' and let herself out of the door.

Janice, silently taking it all in, leaned against the sink. Her aunt had gone back upstairs to make sure she'd not missed anything in her haste to pack.

'Nasty accident, eh?' Janice enquired as I prepared, with some difficulty, lunch and a pot of tea for myself.

'Very,' I agreed.

'Sylvia reckons you were driven off the road, is that right?'

'Almost,' I sighed and I waved her over to a chair by the kitchen table. 'You're going to print this anyway, aren't you?' I said with sudden insight.

'Well, it's just a filler really. Probably on page six, "The People's Page", we're doing a piece on over-crowded motorways. I've already started work on a column about the Calderton Aid Convoy. You've probably seen the adverts...' She glanced pointedly at a pile of black binliners in a corner of the room. Baby clothes poked out of the top. 'Though I must admit it's been a nightmare trying to set up an interview. Megan Jones keeps putting me off. I must have left a dozen messages. I can't even find out who's organising it. Silly bitch. You'd think she'd welcome the publicity, wouldn't you?' She dragged her fingers through a fashionably unruly crop of auburn hair.

'Have you tried visiting the old tyre place on Halifax Road?' I asked thoughtfully.

'It was shut,' she replied. 'Plenty of black bags outside, though.' And she looked at AnnaMaria's pile again. 'Why?'

'Well, it's something Gaz and Darren were on about. Just today as a matter of fact. Do you know them?'

'Gaz and Darren?' She smiled. 'I know *of* them.'

I told her about our brief conversation.

'Worth a look,' she said. 'Small potatoes though.'

'Better than no potatoes at all.'

She fiddled with her hair again. It sprang up in right angles all over her head. She'd probably paid a fortune for the effect. 'Anyway, your accident. We can't say too much. Lots of "alleged" and "sources say", you know the score. East Brook Health Club headlines on Thursday's edition and tonight's is full of the prison escapee that's been spotted near Halifax, though that's likely to be alleged this and alleged that as well . . .'

I leaned forward, prompted once more into curiosity. 'Tell me about it,' I said, and she did, in detail.

'Lorna Thompson was the driver for the gang. The rest of them are dead, by the way,' she said, matter of factly. 'Killed in a smash on the A6. I couldn't believe she only got four years. Her father's a retired QC – '

'I know,' I interrupted and suddenly wished I hadn't.

'You know her?'

'No.'

'But you know of her? From the news? More than that? Come on, Letty. I know you know something. And trust me, if *you* don't tell me, I'll find out one way or another.'

So, obtaining a promise not to do some sort of exposé, I told Janice the story of my narrow escape on the motorway and an extremely censored version of my tenuous connection to Lorna Thompson, late of Styal prison.

I could tell that it had taken every steel nerve in Janice's body not to produce a pad and pen. But her mind was like an encyclopaedia, and the information would be filed away somewhere.

Janice thoughtfully rubbed a leather-booted toe against the stone-tiled kitchen floor. 'Do you think your mother might . . . ?'

'Oh no. No *way*.' The thought filled me with dread. Mum had sworn me to silence. Imagine her reaction if she thought I'd blabbed to the *papers*?

'Yes, but I know her, sort of. Maybe she'd give me an – '

'Don't, Janice. This isn't the world of the *Sun*, you know. And Lorna Thompson has only "allegedly" been sighted as you pointed out yourself. Mountains from molehills, remember?'

Janice pinched her nose between two fingers, sighed and changed the subject. 'This health club thing seems to have taken off at the speed of sound, doesn't it? I've never seen building work like it, well, except for that estate that was chucked up outside Halifax last year. Your mate Stan says most of it is 'ready made' – false walls, ready built saunas, all on wheels at the back of the house. Same with the stables. They've put it together in a couple of weeks. I bet they could take it apart in a day if they had to,' she probed, none too subtly.

'Well, except for the kitchen,' I interrupted, falling for it. 'There's nothing impermanent about that.'

Janice waited. I let her carry on waiting.

'However it's been built,' I relented finally, 'it must have cost thousands. Surely it's a long-term investment.'

'You tell me. You're the one that's visited, and you know Chris Crozier. My aunt told me all about it, in case you were wondering.' She took a moment to pour herself tea, raising a questioning eyebrow at me. I pushed my cup over for a refill. 'She's somebody else I would really like to interview, you know. The *Echo* didn't even get an invite to the opening. No room for us with all the big shots there. *Hello* and *OK!* must have been scratching each other's eyes out. We're having to cover it all by word of mouth. Somebody else's words, somebody else's mouth.' She chuckled.

'I can get you in,' I offered. 'Maybe it's just an oversight. Anyway, I've got connections,' I said with a tired grin.

135

'Anybody I know? Anybody I *ought* to know?'

'Chief cook and bottle washer, literally! Sarah Flowers was working for my mother's fiancé in Scotland. Coincidentally she's working next door now.' Somehow I couldn't resist an explanation. Janice should have been a counsellor, such was the urge to spill what I knew.

'Christ, your life seems to be laden with coincidences lately.' She paused. 'Don't you think?'

Of course I'd thought. Did she think I was stupid?

I made a suggestion. 'You could turn up incognito. You might see more that way.'

Sylvia clattered downstairs with her bags at that point and Janice, leaning across the table, muttered quietly, 'I'll take you up on your offer, but don't tell *her*,' – cocking a thumb in her aunt's direction – 'at least not until you have to, otherwise I'll never hear the last of it.' She turned away from me as Sylvia came through the door. 'Give me your bag, Aunty, I'll give you a lift to the shop.'

Chapter 20

Chris Crozier had obviously hired the same firm that organised the State Opening of Parliament, despite the fact that the press, or at least the *local* press had been excluded. There were plenty of expensive cameras and passes for the quality glossies on show when we arrived at East Brook Health Club that Friday. The bloke from *This Yorkshire Life* had taken one look at our group, decided we weren't quite what he wanted on the centre spread and had instead taken off after a trio of fit but ghostlike women in House of Fraser summer outfits and hats Cilla wouldn't be seen dead in. I knew the type. I'd encountered them at every gym Anne had ever dragged me into. Strong, tall, long, long hair and bottles of Evian hanging from every orifice. They were perpetually thirty, perpetually moist, from the dampest of upper lips to the delicate sheen on their hairless, treadmill-fit calves. Tanned, too. All year round. Jealous? Believe it.

It was a beautiful summer's afternoon. The sun, shrouded in the gentlest grey haze, shone down from a perfectly blue sky, with only fronds of white clouds hundreds of feet in the air.

A long line of trestle tables heaved with food. The

carrot soup and endless salads that Sarah Flowers was convinced were the only things she would ever have to prepare were relegated to one small corner of the spread. Every conceivable canapé and dip, starter and nibble, were stretched across the expanse of midnight-blue linen tablecloth. Sarah must have been up all night. She should have given me a knock.

A crew of bar staff clad in white polo necks had taken charge of the drinks tables and several young women in black trouser suits, narrow ties and waistcoats beneath their ankle-length aprons scurried to and from the house; collecting, delivering and arranging food and plates.

Liam's eyes lit up. He knew a feast when he saw one. He took off, clutching Andy's hand and AnnaMaria's sleeve, and elbowed his way through the chattering crowd to leave the rest of our party in limbo on the lawn.

I'd taken Chris Crozier's invitation to 'bring a friend, hell, bring them all!' to heart. Alongside AnnaMaria, Mrs Buckham and Janice was Sita, who had a spare afternoon before she visited her niece. Julia would be along later. Sita, exhausted by travel and entertainment, was missing her lover but, even so, could only manage a few hours off.

My mother had arrived earlier in the day in my repaired Land Rover, en route for a brief visit to her home. She'd declined the offer of an afternoon fête but had stayed at the farm long enough to convince herself that I was, in fact, fully recovered from my accident.

'I feel so guilty,' she'd said for the umpteenth time. 'If only I'd let you wait for the AA. I should have had the car checked, but it seemed so reliable. It had only been serviced in January and the mechanics hadn't pointed out any problems.' She was near to tears. 'You don't think it was deliberate, do you?' Mum asked after a short pause.

I shook my head. 'An unfortunate combination of circumstances.' I'd had time to think about things and a good dose of farming reality had put my mind at ease. Almost completely. The BMW was still in Carlisle and despite my mother mithering the police, no inspection had yet been made.

'I went to see it, you know,' she said.

I cringed, I knew what was coming. My account of the accident had been somewhat toned down, though I couldn't deny the car was kaput.

'Letitia,' she choked. '*There was nothing left*. It was completely burned out. If it hadn't have been for the number plate, I wouldn't even have recognised it as mine.'

'I know,' I said uncomfortably. 'I didn't want to worry you . . .'

Mum grabbed my arm and gave me one of her fierce looks, though she didn't say anything.

'Have you seen the police?' she'd asked at last. 'Since the accident?'

I'd explained that I had an appointment in the week. WPC Emma would be taking a statement, having a chat, cross-examining me, whatever.

'And the motorway cameras? Any news there? Have they tracked down those lorry drivers?'

I shook my head, 'I suppose the police have got more important things to worry about.' I considered telling her that the escapee had been spotted in the area, but decided against it. The police knew and Mum had enough on her plate, why add to her worries? Anyway, if it was Lorna, then the further away from Scotland she was, the better.

Mum had taken my hand across the kitchen table and smiled wanly. 'You're my daughter, what could be more important?'

'What about you?' I asked hurriedly. 'Any more phone calls?'

Mum looked away. 'One. Silent again.'

'Tell the police,' I urged gently. She smiled and shook her head. I'd offered her a lift home, but she said she'd get the train. She had a hire car lined up. An Audi TT this time, in millennium silver. Despite my misfortune on the motorway, my mum hadn't been put off fast cars.

'I'll be heading back to Scotland for a few days soon. Why don't you come with me? Take a break, your hands must still be sore.'

I declined her offer, and though I was concerned for Mum, Scotland held no appeal. Selfishly I couldn't see myself visiting in the foreseeable future. I took her to the local station and she left, a tad disappointed.

I had a phone call that morning too. Sylvia Buckham, the only woman I knew who got up earlier than I did. I think I expected a thank you for putting her up. But no. I got a complaint, well, a moan really.

'I've been up all night,' she bellowed down the phone.

'Why?'

'The shop. That Frankie Field and his worthless family. Half the floorboards were still up. Nearly broke my neck when I went over the threshold. Janice says she'll sue him once she gets her hands on him. You can't trust anybody,' she raged.

I'd let her go on for a while, commenting 'oh dear' and 'that's shocking' in all the right places until she'd calmed down a bit. I'd then asked her if she wanted to come back to the farm until the shop was sorted.

'Oh, it's all fixed,' she said. 'Your AnnaMaria's Andy helped out, and those two boys, they're not all bad after all,' she explained. 'Shame there aren't more like them in the village.'

Eventually, she'd rung off.

By now it was three o'clock and Christine's party was in full swing. Crowds of people were arriving at the Health Club; cash on the Gucci-clad hoof. I'd once had a car auction on my farm and I'd not seen so many loaded people in one place since. Chris Crozier Junior, decked out in a sparkly, spangly trouser suit, hair blonder than ever, charged over to us as we deliberated over the food.

'Letty, honey!' she bellowed. 'You made it. Welcome, one and all,' she said to my friends. She looked closely at Sita, took in her beautifully designed, Eastern-style dress, and the regal stance. At five foot ten Sita had an effortless elegance that turned heads, and so much poise it was almost illegal. 'Sita Joshi!' she pronounced loudly. 'Hell, lady. I betchya don't remember me!'

We all looked at Sita whose face was thoughtful, then puzzled, before recognition began to dawn. She avoided an 'oh no' look of horror by a whisker, recovering smoothly with a cool, 'I thought your name was familiar,' a smile and the offer of an outstretched hand. Chris grabbed at it and pumped it up and down. There was no immediate sign that she'd ever let go.

'I swear this planet gets smaller and smaller,' she crowed. Hands continued to be raised and lowered vigorously; one dark one clutched in a pink and unrelenting grip. 'What was it? Four, five years ago now?' The up and down motion slowed and finally stopped. Sita's hand remained clenched, not quite to the point of discomfort, but not far off. Chris's smile was fixed, too wide, too *telling* somehow.

Something was happening here, but I had no idea what.

She turned to the rest of us. 'Sita here came to visit my daddy in Texas to discuss his business, a while ago now. Britain was just getting involved with this prison privatisation idea and you and your colleagues wanted to see how it worked. You weren't very impressed, if I remember.' Her head drifted to one side, every word and the wide-eyed expression, a challenge.

Chris, I was beginning to discover, blew as hot and cold as her father.

Sita shook her head. 'It's not something I agreed with and I still don't, to be honest. Public security isn't something that should have a profit margin, in my opinion.'

'It didn't stop it happening though,' Chris responded, the flash of a grin doing nothing to soften the words. 'And my daddy is very happy with his profit margins, I think.'

'Despite recent problems and the questions that have been raised?' Sita rejoined. A thin film of ice covered the question and a thicker one quickly settled on my stomach with Chris's astonishing reply.

'Escapes come with the territory, honey.' Our hostess glanced around, suddenly bored with it all. 'Anyway, this is a party. Only the horses are locked up here. Get a drink, have some food. But if you want to thrash it out some more, my daddy's here somewhere.' She laughed, turned to me and hooked her arm in mine. 'I'm going to steal you for a few minutes,' she whispered. 'If your friends don't mind.' I began to protest, I suddenly had urgent questions for the MP, but I was already in Chris's vicelike grip.

'I might not get a chance to see you later,' Sita called, relieved to see her partner trudging down the path. 'I've got to make tracks soon.' She scurried off clutching a paper plate full of half-eaten food.

Janice was waggling her fingers at me. 'Catch you later,' she said and off she went to mingle with, or perhaps quiz, the other guests. She had Amy, Megan Jones and her secretary, Sue, already in her sights.

Reluctantly I allowed myself to be dragged away.

Chris released my arm, reached up around my shoulder and gave me a powerful squeeze. It was like being hugged by a thin but wiry orang-utan. She led me through the crowd.

Occasionally I caught a 'Chris, hi!', or 'Fantastic place. Do you do a group discount?' and a cascade of laughter would drift our way. Chris smiled beatifically at her audience and whispered to me through her teeth, 'Hardly know a goddamn one of these people. Which hole did they crawl out of?'

We stepped across the spongy grass, skirting the crowds, and headed towards Chris's house.

'So who invited them?' I asked, still cautious around this strange woman.

'My daddy, who else?' She sighed, a slight edge of bitterness to her words. 'That's the trouble with these informal partnerships, one hand doesn't know what the other's doing.' We edged nearer the house, Chris's powerful arm still draped around me. 'Your injuries healing okay now, honey? Got over the worst of the shock?'

I glanced at my fingers. Scabs and white scar tissue (where I'd picked at the itchy scabs) still showed. My ripped nails were giving me problems, though Chris didn't seem to be someone I could moan to about that.

'Fine,' I said.

'Good,' she said and hugged me harder. 'Let me get you a drink. And I believe a friend of yours wants to see you.'

'Oh?'

'Sarah said to point you in the direction of the kitchen when I got a chance. That lady's got a soft spot for you,' she added unexpectedly.

As thrilled as that comment made me feel, I felt obliged to quiz Chris before she had chance to head back. She looked at me, a bland expression on her face. 'Yes, honey?'

'I don't know what to make of you,' I confessed.

She frowned, looking perplexed. 'Why?'

I blundered into the conversation. 'You know about Sarah. You obviously now know about me . . .'

'Of course. And Julia, and your ex. Anne, wasn't she called? I also know everything I ever need to know about the village, its inhabitants, and all the wheeling and dealing that the folks indulge in. Possibly more than even you're aware of. Does that surprise you?'

'No,' I said faintly. 'Amazed might be nearer. Amazed . . .' My voice got a little stronger. 'And annoyed perhaps.'

She sighed and ran her hand through her hair, a little irritated now. 'Look,' she said. 'A big investment has been made in this place and no doubt a hell of a lot more cash will be spent before it's finished. My father likes to know what he's paying his money into, and what he's likely to get in return –'

'And checking up on your neighbours seemed like a good idea, did it?' I interrupted.

Chris went on as though I'd never spoken. 'And knowing *who* and *what* your neighbours are is a good

144

start. But I'm not judgemental, I don't give a damn about your screwy British habits.' She yanked out her hairband and tossed her silky hair back. 'Despite what Amy thinks.'

'Oh,' I said, surprised all over again.

'Honey,' she said quietly, 'I don't miss a trick.' And she shoved her hair behind her ears and wandered back to her party.

Chapter 21

Sarah was laughing hard by the time I'd finished with my tale of affronted sensibilities.

'It's not funny,' I insisted. 'It's a bloody cheek.'

Sarah roared. 'It *is* funny. Hysterical even. I wish I could have seen her face.'

'I suppose you got the same treatment then. She'll know all about you too.'

'Well, she thinks she does,' Sarah said mysteriously, and she looked away, bringing a bottle of beer to her lips.

'What do you know about her?' I asked curiously.

Sarah shrugged. 'Only what's on show.'

'And her dad?'

'Same with him.'

'Julia's girlfriend met him once, you know. Something about privatising prisons.' I thought about Lorna, debating once again the likelihood of a connection. Surely not. Styal wasn't a private prison.

'Well, they don't talk to me about their business,' Sarah said quietly.

My legs dangled either side of the wide fence we were sharing, and I took another sandwich from the plate she'd thoughtfully brought with her to our impromptu picnic.

Sarah had been waiting for me outside the kitchen door as Chris, still a bit staggered that I'd been offended, pointed out her whereabouts.

'I've done all I can,' Sarah had explained, clutching food and a couple of bottles of chilled Budweiser. 'Pay day stopped half an hour ago. Anyway, there's enough food to feed the five thousand *and* all their relatives. Other people are being paid to dish it up. Come on,' she'd insisted. 'Let's get away from the crowds.'

I let my gaze wander over to the fields in the distance. A few of Stan's sheep were dotted like low-lying white clouds across the skyline.

'It doesn't seem a bit peculiar to you?' I asked.

Sarah took a few seconds to pick out a particularly plump piece of fruit. She was sitting opposite me: we were face to face, a length of fencing and a plate between us.

'You know I said I've worked in some hell-holes?' she asked finally. I nodded. 'Well, I've lived in some as well. I only wish I'd had the opportunity to check out my neighbours first. I'd have rather lived over there with them,' she said, pointing to the flock grazing in the fields.

'Well, it just seemed so weird,' I admitted.

'Worried what she may have found out?' Sarah asked me with a sideways look.

'My life, unfortunately, is an open book. I don't think Julia will be too thrilled when I tell her though. And AnnaMaria, remember? Anne's niece? I can imagine all too clearly what she'll have to say.'

'You could always keep it to yourself.'

147

I grinned and took a swig of the Bud. 'That's probably the best idea you've had.'

Sarah shuffled over towards me and suddenly, but gently, removed the bottle from my grasp.

'This is a better one,' she said and leaned over, put her unoccupied hand behind my head and pulled me towards her. She kissed me. The sort of long, hard and passionate kiss I'd almost forgotten existed. Soft, soft lips found mine, and I could feel those unyielding, slightly crooked teeth in a mouth that I'd wanted, but hadn't allowed myself to expect. I sensed a loss of any control I may have had as her hand buried itself fiercely in my hair. Ten seconds of that and I was helpless. She pulled away and looked at me. Those honey eyes asked a question that I was too stunned to answer.

She took my hand, abandoned our picnic at the base of the fence and led me away. We left behind neighbours I'd known for years, friends who would have had some raucous comments to make, a group of complete strangers, and headed towards the shelter and seclusion of a cluster of weeping willows. I don't suppose I need to paint a picture of what happened next, do I?

I took memories of my new lover to my appointment with Calderton's only policewoman. Thoughts of Sarah's firm and slightly possessive touch distracted me enough to make me forget some of the stuff I should probably have shared with the woman who sat opposite me in the interview room. Sex, I discovered, makes you stupid.

I assumed Emma knew all about Lorna Thompson so I didn't bother to remind her. I omitted to tell her about Mum's suspicious phone calls. I glossed over the fact that I shouldn't have been driving my mother's car at all. The knowledge that the police investigation in Carlisle was inconclusive – they couldn't prove that the car had either been tampered with or had a basic mechanical flaw – washed over me the same way Sarah's hands had washed over my body. I was as useful as an ashtray on a motorbike.

Still, Emma took notes, enquired after the insurance (the pursuit of which I'd left in my mother's capable hands), and asked, oddly enough, about CFC Inspirational Health and Beauty.

This I could tell her. *That* memory would stay with me for ever. After I'd given her a fairly insightful summary of CFC's running and Chris's leadership I asked her if she'd visited yet.

'Not been invited,' she said gruffly. 'And I've no time, no inclination.'

She was obviously just being nosy then.

The interview was almost over when I remembered something.

'Did the motorway cameras pick anything up, you know, about the crash?'

'Vandalised,' she said and left it at that.

Janice was sitting on my doorstep hugging her denim-clad knees when I got home. Honestly, I may as well get a key cut for the whole village.

There was a racket going on next door and I shimmied up the stepladder to see what was going on. A big van was noisily delivering something. No, some*one*. Several someones actually, each dragging a big valise, the sort that probably sunk with the *Titanic*. Guests, perhaps? No sign of Sarah, though.

Janice called me and I returned to my house.

'I need a favour,' she stated as I opened the door.

'No time,' I said and threw my car keys onto the table. 'I'm meeting somebody.' Somebody I hoped to be shagging before the day was out.

'It's important,' she said. So's Sarah, I thought. 'And I've got something to tell you that you really need to know.'

'What?'

'I'll tell you on the way. Help me out here, Letty, please. It'll take an hour or two, maybe a bit less. I just need you to take some photos.'

'Me? Why? Is your camera broken?'

'No, I want you to use mine. Come on, Letty, it's not very often I ask a favour.'

That statement wasn't entirely true.

I rinsed my hands at the sink and wondered whether to get changed. Sarah was taking me out for a meal. I'd be as fat as a pig if this went on for long. Every time I saw her she plyed me with something. A small, dirty thought arose and I could feel my neck flush with the memory.

After our tête-à-tête in the field under the protective arms of the weeping willows, I decided that this was one worth pursuing. So far it was sex, something I'd been denied for too long. But Sarah was nice, generous, sexy and forceful in a breathtaking way that I wasn't used to, but wouldn't mind *getting* used to.

I checked the kitchen clock. I could spare an hour or so and I was curious as to Janice's news.

'Okay. What do you want me to do?'

Chapter 22

We drew up about a half mile from our destination and got out of Janice's battered Metro.

I carefully finished fiddling with Janice's Nikon. A sudden, hollow, 'this is going to end so badly' feeling caused stomach acids to over-react. I tried to ignore the sensation.

Darren and Gaz were waiting by the side of the deserted road leaning against a big blue Cadillac. There was only one like it in the area. It was probably the only one for fifty miles in any direction.

AnnaMaria had told me all about it after my first run-in with the boys. She'd worked on the car herself a number of times. The big V8 engine, which was about as old as AnnaMaria, needed a lot of attention; attention Darren's father, a strict middle-aged man who was employed on the oil rigs for most of the year, couldn't always give it. And here it was, on a dusty back road five miles from home with no sign of its owner.

It took me all of two seconds to realise that Darren had driven it himself. My overworked stomach fizzed some more.

'Janice,' I said in alarm. 'Why are those two here?'

'Oh, you'll see,' she replied.

The boys were both dressed in black: black trainers, black jeans, black T-shirts and Nike beanie hats. Their faces were covered in dark green camouflage paint. It was a bright, warm summer's afternoon and they blended into their surroundings like a ginger tom in the middle of a snowstorm.

Janice merely sighed.

'Now you both know what to do, don't you?'

'Yeah, cool,' Darren said excitedly.

Gaz held his palm out and Janice dug around in a pocket. Money exchanged hands.

'How long have you been here?' Janice asked the boys.

'Twenty minutes,' Darren replied.

'And no movement?'

Darren shook his head.

'Come on then, let's see what we can see.'

The two boys both possessed mobile phones, so communication wouldn't be a problem. Darren was left near the car as an early warning signal. He'd brought a camcorder with him, the origins of which, like the phones, I didn't want to enquire about. Whatever Janice expected to happen would be caught on film.

Janice's back was up, hence this little jaunt. She'd tracked down Megan Jones at the launch of the Health Club and had spent an hour trying to pin her down about the Aid Convoy. Megan, apparently, had been her usual evasive self. The more evasive she was, the more persistent was Janice. And Janice wasn't a woman to be denied. Sue, the put-upon and generally unappreciated secretary, had been much more forthcoming. The conversation had made it clear that the garage was worth investigating. Megan had been twitchy since the Aid Convoy had been announced and Sue, an increasingly unhappy secretary with access to telephone extensions and private files, had been left with a few suspicions herself. Nothing she could put her finger on, but *something* told her all was not as it seemed.

'And why did Sue tell you all this?' I asked. 'What happened to loyalty, eh?'

'Loyalty? My arse,' Janice snorted. 'Sue didn't get a pay rise, a promotion *or* a place on the advanced IT course she'd been promised. Not a happy bunny, that one.'

And what expertise did I have to offer this little caper? I was there to take pictures of the inside of the garage. Gaz was on hand as lookout and to get us through the back door that he'd done a recce on earlier in the day. Janice's marbles definitely needed a tweak.

Halifax Tyre and Tread was a huge corrugated iron structure last used as a garage years before I'd moved to Calderton. It had been taken over by a local youth club until the council condemned it. Garage pits were deemed unsuitable for kids who had no concept of danger. Darren, who'd not had a qualm about driving a car Jeremy Clarkson would find a little hot to handle, being a prime example.

Me, Gaz and Janice made our way towards the building by a back route. The surrounding fields were still, but only just, farmland. A track of sorts, desperately kept open by a local Ramblers' Association, led a circuitous route past. The path was flanked by huge weeds and blackberry bushes; bees bounced from flower to flower. The encroaching vegetation had turned the path into a sun trap – it was a good five degrees hotter than on open land. A slight westerly breeze had brought with it high temperatures all the way from the Sahara.

I knew it would be a short-lived weatherfront, Radio 4 had promised squally showers later in the week, but for the moment the sun's undiluted rays were beating down on the three of us and Gaz's warpaint was beginning to melt.

Having forgotten my watch, I had a quick guess at the time. We'd already been pissing about for at least half an hour. If I was late for my date, Janice would pay.

The reporter ordered Gaz forward on point duty. 'He's loving this,' she said with a smile.

I was pleased that somebody was.

'Not far now,' she said as if I was new to the area. Gaz disappeared round a corner and was hidden from sight by a vast and ancient oak tree that had been climbed by generations of Yorkshire children and peed on by generations of Yorkshire dogs.

I sighed, louder than I'd intended and Janice, wiping sweat from her brow, turned to look at me. 'What?' she asked.

'What exactly are you hoping to do?' I blurted. 'What are a few photos and the sworn statements of a couple of fifteen-year-old hooligans, who shouldn't be here in the first place, going to prove? It's a charity for God's sake!'

As usual, when things got tricky, she didn't answer.

'I mean, just what is Sue's gripe? There are wild goose chases and then there's stupidity,' I raged, suddenly too hot and too bothered. 'What sort of scam does she think's going on?' Her silence irritated me even more. '*Janice*,' I insisted.

'Look,' she said finally and stared up at me. Sweat dampened her upper lip and a great dimpled frown appeared between her eyes. 'She just thinks it's some sort of fiddle. I don't know, maybe with donations or government grants or something. Even I can't find out who's funding the damn operation. Nobody knows anything. And Sue reckons that somebody, somewhere is making a packet.'

'What, and the police have retired, have they?'

'Oh, that's rich coming from you. All the trouble you've had in the past and who're the last people you ring, eh?'

I was silent. She was right. I had similar misgivings to Mrs Buckham's. The police had tended to bring more trouble to my door, not less.

'Anyway, who's to say the police aren't involved? Mmm?'

We'd jumped from Sue's vague suspicions to a conspiracy theory.

'All I can suggest is that you either stick with it a bit, or go home,' she snapped.

Needless to say, I stuck with it.

We passed the oak tree and there was still no sign of Gaz. The tyre place was less than fifty feet away and great blank walls, stained brown in places by harsh winters, towered over us. There'd been some half-hearted attempt to clear the encircling overgrowth but the building was old and uninviting, cheerless even on a summer's day. And it was in far more urgent need of a makeover than either Julia's garage, which was a few miles away, or Mrs Buckham's shop.

The place looked abandoned. Piles of plastic bags, binliners and green refuse sacks were stacked against the dingy walls. Gusts of wind had upended some of them and tiny T-shirts and miniature vests hung from nearby bushes. There was an air of loss and rejection about the clothes, as though nobody, not even those most in need, wanted anything to do with them.

*

We found Gaz by the back, his head already craned around the narrowly opened doorway. He heard us coming and waved us down into a crouch. He'd obviously watched too many films.

We scrambled over and both my knees popped loudly in the silence. Gaz cracked the door open a little wider. 'It was already open,' he tried to convince us, though the misshapen lock told me otherwise. 'There's nobody about.'

'So why are we whispering?' I asked evenly.

'Shh!' my companions chorused.

Janice and I took a quick peek. The back door led directly into an office. A large room, maybe fifteen foot by twelve, enclosed by dirty three-quarter-height glass, overlooked the rest of the structure. It was silent, deserted, filthy. Several metal filing cabinets, in Civil Service grey, lined one wall and a desk, obviously from the same source, occupied the centre of the room. A large industrial sewing machine, threaded with bright cotton, was sat on top. I speculated that maybe they repaired the clothes before shipping them out. A foldaway bed, covered in a once white sheet, was stacked neatly in the furthest corner. The tremendous heat hit me then, that and the smell of warm rubber and unwashed bodies.

Gaz looked at Janice and bubbles of sweat popped out across the bridge of his painted, acned nose. He made strange finger gestures with his right hand which could have meant anything at all, and he suddenly took off, crabbing his way across the office floor.

Janice unshrugged a record bag from her shoulder, gently ripped open the velcro fastening and produced an electronic hand-held device. A tiny red light throbbed relentless as a pulse at its top right-hand corner. *Rank*

Xerox was printed in italic subscript below it. She pressed a couple of buttons and, as a thousand microchips powered up, the black plastic object clicked into life.

I got as far as, 'What is...' before Janice shushed me to silence for the second time. And, having attended the same assault course as Gaz, she shuffled across the floor beckoning me onwards with finger gestures even I could understand. I got a close-up of ancient oil stains, nails that had worked their way out of cracked and decaying floorboards and the sparse remains of the type of paint that would probably be illegal now. I tried not to breathe too deeply.

Finally I reached my compadres by the filing cabinet. As shabby as the floor, the metal was chipped and rusted in places, and most of the drawers were missing a screw or two. Like Janice, I thought to myself, and giggled nervously.

'Shush' Janice gestured wildly. She waggled her index finger. What was that supposed to mean?

'Go on,' she said, exasperated. 'Pictures, snap snap. Point and press.' She yanked thin latex gloves over each hand.

'Less of the sarcasm, you,' I muttered back. 'And what the hell are you doing with those?' I jabbed a finger at the flesh-toned surgical accessories. 'You still haven't told me what I'm supposed to be taking pictures of,' I persisted. This little excursion had seemed so harmless a couple of hours ago.

The reporter put her little machine to her ear and gave it a shake. 'Take whatever,' she replied. 'Gaz'll show you.'

'Gaz'll get us all arrested. Do you know how old he is? Corrupting a minor, that's what this is. Breaking and entering –'

'We didn't break, we just entered.'

'Don't tell me you didn't notice the lock on the back door, Janice. Because I don't believe it! Not to mention damage to personal property.' I gasped as Janice, with an industrial-sized flat-head screwdriver, started work on one of the locked drawers of the filing cabinet.

'Go!' she ordered.

I unslung the camera from around my neck, managed not to crack her over the head with it, and followed orders.

I joined Gaz in a crouch below the glass ledge of the flimsy office wall. A three-foot hardboard wall protected us from any prying eyes he may have missed on his first assault on the premises. Janice, having personally reached the breaking stage of breaking and entering, managed to force one of the drawers open. She barely stifled a shriek of pain as the metal crashed into her midriff. Gaz laughed and I hoped any prying eyes were between two deaf ears. Gaz popped his head above the sill and without looking back he folded his bony fingers around my forearm and pulled me up with him.

Big as it was, I could still take in the whole building with one quick glance. Its lower level was easily reached by a short wooden staircase, with a flimsy rail on either side. A three-legged pool table and an ancient dartboard, still hanging from a wall, were the only evidence left of youth club activity.

At the end of the room were huge double doors, big enough for a tractor, a Range Rover and possibly a tank to drive through. They were closed and a long metal bar wedged across them ensured they would stay that way.

To the left was a smaller, human-sized doorway.

'We're going down,' Gaz hissed at Janice.

She waved a quick acknowledgement, her interest

now absorbed by the contents of the cabinet. She spread sheets of paper across the floor and ran her little machine across the face of each one.

'Wow, get that scanner,' Gaz breathed in my ear.

'What the hell is she up to?' I muttered.

'Some weird shit she won't tell me about,' Gaz said cheerfully. 'Got the camera ready?' he asked.

I nodded nervously, mouth suddenly as dry as a *Newsnight* panel.

'Come on then.'

It was even hotter in the main part of the garage. A huge black Mercedes van, sporting last year's registration, was up on an industrial jack in the process of having a new tyre fitted. Its twin was parked over a garage pit. They were in excellent condition and would have no problem with a gruelling trek across Europe.

Their headlights caught my gaze. Yellow plastic covers had been fixed. The type required for the continent. AID CONVOY had been recently freshly stencilled across the side panels. Things were hanging together just right as far as I could make out.

A dirty mug, the tea still steaming, sat among a pile of greasy tools on the edge of a garage pit. I pointed this out to Gaz.

'If he's just gone for a piss, well, he won't be long will he?' he stated with a shrug. Gaz was proving to be a cool dude under pressure. He wasn't fazed by our illegal presence. 'Come on,' he urged. 'Get snapping.'

With a few more years in the bag, I was less easily impressed.

'Snap?' I snapped. 'Snap what?'

'Anything, everything!' His camouflage paint which, judging from the smell, had come from his mother's makeup case (green and black – should I be worrying about his mother?) had started to streak down his neck.

My barely healed fingers began to throb. Any breath I took didn't seem to reach my lungs and the combined aromas of hot rubber, cheap cosmetics, sweat (my own included), and a smell that was akin to trenchfoot, were all threatening to make me lose my lunch.

Gaz didn't seem to notice either my anxiety or the putrid odours and, clutching my arm again, he dragged me over for a closer look at the truck parked above the pit.

The Merc's roller door at the back was half open and, to Gaz at least, very inviting. He stuck his head underneath to get a closer look. After a moment he reappeared. 'We need more light,' he whispered. He grabbed the door and heaved. It slid open to reveal piles and piles of rugs, blankets and duvets. Somebody, somewhere would be glad of this lot and for a second I was relieved. We'd proved our point, disproved Sue's, and we could go home.

Gaz hooked his foot onto the tail-gate and reached for the grab handle.

'Do you have objections to humanitarian aid?' I asked him, relief turning to dread. My sarcasm went screaming over his head.

'Oh, stop moaning,' he said. 'And help me up.'

I gave him a shove, juggling the camera with one hand. He landed on his knees in the back of the van and turned to offer me a hand. I grabbed his outstretched arm and ended up sprawled across the metal floor.

A jumble sale aroma hit my nostrils. I got to my feet. The truck was piled high, blankets towered way over my head. Strong bungee-type ropes held most of them firmly in place. Others, in the process of being packed for the journey, were still loosely stacked.

I reached over to run my hands across the blankets and, suddenly curious, I attempted to pull one up. Several, of different yarns and colours, all came up together.

'Funny,' I said half to myself.

'What is?'

I turned to Gaz. 'Look, they're all stitched together. I wonder why?' I whispered. Gaz moved in for a closer look and grabbed another bundle.

'Same here,' he said. He crushed the material in his wiry hands. 'Listen,' he said and held the blanket near my ear. An odd crinkly, crackling sound emanated from the cloth. 'Got a knife or owt?' he asked looking around the van.

I reached in my back pocket. I had a Swiss Army knife attached to my keys. 'Here.'

Gaz glanced at me and grinned, impressed. He sawed away at the material for a minute. It wouldn't give. 'Try the stitching,' I urged, now intrigued rather than nervous.

The cotton finally came apart. A bundle of twenty pound notes cascaded to the floor.

'Fuck me,' he said in wonder.

'Oh my God,' I replied and unthinkingly took a photo.

Gaz, blinking against the glare, shoved an arm between the blankets and produced a fistful of cash. Our eyes met in the half light.

'It's stuffed with *money*,' he exclaimed.

I would have been less surprised if he'd produced a rabbit.

In seconds his black jeans were crammed with bank notes. 'Wish I'd worn me combats,' he said excitedly.

'Gaz,' I warned. He ignored me. 'Put it back.'

'Yeah, right,' he said. His pockets bulged and he looked around for another receptacle. 'How deep are *your* pockets?'

Suddenly my mind was full of images of Chilean drug smugglers, Mafia hitmen and Russian gangsters. I closed my eyes, briefly, against potential outcomes. 'We shouldn't mess with this,' I said and made a grab for his bulging back pocket. The thick double-stitched denim was subject to a brief but fierce tug of war – a war I was never going to win.

'No *way*!' Gaz hissed, suddenly more subdued than he'd been all day.

'Take pictures,' he said, pulling away. 'That's what you're here for.'

'Have you any idea whose –'

'I don't bleedin' care whose it is. Look, just take the pictures. I'll split the dosh with you if you're *that* bothered.'

'I don't want the money. I just don't want to get caught.'

Too amazed to do much else, I took pictures, plus some experimental ones where I stuck the lens directly among the blankets. A thought occurred: if the mechanic had gone to the toilet, it must be the longest visit ever.

Gaz suddenly reached into his jacket and produced a vibrating but silent mobile phone.

'Foxtrot,' he whispered into the mouthpiece and, after a moment, 'Tango. Foxtrot out.'

'Come on,' he urged, gently replacing his phone. 'There's somebody coming.' He snatched the camera from my hand and shoved me towards the back of the van. We jumped out, clattering too loudly against the concrete, and raced breathlessly, terrified, past piles of stitched together blankets, tyres and assorted garage equipment.

A noise from the front door and Gaz's hands were

squarely in the middle of my back. He shoved me head first behind an old wooden desk. Cleverly I managed to land on both elbows leaving enough DNA evidence for even the most witless of Kay Scarpetta wannabes. The tabletop, supported by two surviving legs, was at precisely the right angle to keep us safe from view.

Gaz dived behind me, and, as the dust settled, the front door crashed open.

Slowly Gaz took a peek above the overturned desk. 'Mechanic's back,' he mouthed. We were situated directly below Janice and her filing cabinet. I could make out the soft shuffle of papers being sorted, the high-pitched whine of the scanner. Raising the camera above his head so slowly a Tai Chi teacher would have been impressed, Gaz tapped the long unwieldy lens against the glass of the upstairs office. The paper shuffling stopped, and the whine was silenced.

Nothing moved for a long time. Our ears strained in the oily, heated silence. And then in the distance I think only I caught the soft but less than subtle creak of a door hinge. Janice, it was clear, had left the building.

Eventually, after a few more nervy moments, the mechanic clattered further into the garage, pushing something across the floor. Gaz and I stared at each other, breathing the putrid air ever more shallowly, ever more quietly.

The old wooden desk protecting us from view had started to separate at the joins. The glue holding it together had become as opaque and thin as glass, leaving an eyeball-sized peephole just within my reach. I edged towards it and huge drops of sweat plopped from my forehead onto the back of my hand. I blinked quickly to stop the salty liquid from dripping into my eyes and peered through the gap.

Red hair and bandaged face were the decisive clues. Liz. Last seen in Mrs Buckham's shop juggling joinery equipment.

I sucked in a sharp, shocked breath. I don't know who I'd been expecting but it certainly wasn't Liz. What in God's name was she up to?

I looked closer. I could see some of the bandages had been replaced with plasters. Yellowed and faded bruises stretched almost from ear to ear.

'What can you see?' Gaz asked directly into my ear. 'Let me look.' I shook my head and slapped my hand over his mouth. A piece of the wooden desk, dislodged by my sudden movement, slithered to the floor. A cloud of dust drifted into the air.

Too late. Silence again from the main floor. I risked another peek and Liz's eyes were suddenly fixed on mine. I didn't dare move, didn't dare blink. Gaz sat beside me, as stiff and as silent as a sleeping member of the House of Lords. The staring competition went on and on until, with the sort of luck that had evaded me all of my life, I realised what she was looking at: a small fat mouse had scrambled from beneath a broken chair not three feet away. It paused to check out how the land lay, its nose and whiskers catching the scent of human presence. It did an odd sideways skip, twitched its scarred tail and ran towards a stack of tyres. Liz shrugged and looked away. She snatched up her tea mug and took a swig. I blinked rapidly for ten seconds.

Liz swiped her hand through her hair, the bottle-red lushness of it shining brightly under the intense gleam of the strip lighting. Reaching for her tools she slid into the pit under the chassis of the Mercedes. So she was a mechanic too...

Ratchets were ratched and tappits tapped as Gaz and

I watched and listened in silence. We sat and sweated wondering if the woman was ever going to take another break. An estimated twenty minutes seemed to stretch into bum-numbing, armpit-stinking hours. We continued to suck tainted oxygen.

Finally, prompted into an executive decision, Gaz leaned over once again.

'After three,' he said coolly. 'Then follow me.'

I shook my head violently. I reckoned I could sit here another hour, maybe two, possibly even all night if I had to, and then walk out free and clear. No problem. An index finger was shoved in my face. I shook my head. No, no, no. V for Victory followed.

'Come on, you old dyke,' he whispered and with a grin, he gripped my forearm.

My eyes bulged.

'And three,' he yelled, top note.

He kicked the desk over and hauled me to my feet. I was getting a bit tired of this sort of treatment.

A spanner was dropped in alarm. In seconds, having skilfully manoeuvred our way past rusty objects that would kill quicker than a Komodo dragon, we were parallel to the pit. A pit where two filthy and bony hands were already clawing their way over the sides.

Gaz, jacket flapping behind him, had one hand on me and the other, with Janice's Nikon at the end of it, pointed towards the pit like a gun. As Liz's face appeared over the edge, Gaz flipped a switch on the camera. The 200-watt light took in the van, the woman's open-mouthed look of surprise, and eyes blinded by the sudden flash.

The teenager flung me forward towards the door and the Nikon, set to automatic, flashed again and again in Liz's face. I saw her struggle out of the pit and promptly crash into a blue metal toolbox. I was left with the image of the temporarily sightless mechanic executing a beautiful nosedive into a row of tyres.

Gaz, whooping with the joy of success, was just a breath behind me. He stopped to slam the door shut and jam a monkey wrench he'd somehow aquired across the old-fashioned, open-ended handles, effectively locking it from the outside.

I kept on running. Knees pumping, arms reaching – in such a panic I could have carried on for miles. I passed the space where the Cadillac had been hours before and just kept on going.

Chapter 23

I eventually ran out of steam struggling over a stile that led into nearby fields. Gaz, with an effortless, long-loping stride, jumped over the connecting fence, one hand skimming the wood, to land at my feet.

Acres of rape seed cast a yellowing glow, broken only by the bright green leaves of newly sprouting potatoes.

Gaz, barely out of breath (in sharp contrast to my air-gulping), hoisted himself astride the fence, one eye on the path in case Liz had decided to pursue us.

So far there was no sign of her.

'Top, weren't it?'

I was too exhausted to offer a reply. I leaned over, hands on thighs as a bout of nausea threatened to become something more tangible. My mouth filled with water and my stomach did a ninety degree turn.

'You all right?' he asked. 'Gonna puke?'

I spat on the floor and shook my head as I gained control of my innards. I straightened up. 'I'm okay,' I confirmed.

'Ya look like shit,' he offered. 'Too old for all this.'

'Thanks,' I said, managing at least a little sarcasm.

'You knew her, didn't ya?' he asked slyly. A cautious

yet expectant look beamed through the remains of his warpaint.

'Why?' I responded.

'It were obvious. Written all over yer face.' He paused. 'Who is she then?'

I sighed, but explained.

'Does Janice know her?' he asked.

'Who knows?' I said, but suggested he made certain Janice got to see the pictures pronto.

'And the money? What the fuck do we do about that?'

'Stop swearing,' I said absently as I tried to collect my thoughts. 'I can't believe it.' I shook my head in amazement. 'All that cash. I mean, whose is it? What the hell's going on?'

'Them blankets were *stuffed*. Chocka,' he said.

'I know,' I muttered. 'I saw you help yourself, remember?'

He grinned.

'Anyway, when you see her, make sure you tell Janice. You *will* see her, won't you?'

He nodded. 'That's the plan. If we got separated we'd catch up with her later.'

I was going to ask how, but thought better of it. I was already heading towards denial.

'I'm sure she'll let the cops know,' I went on, but realised that once Janice was onto a story she'd do no such thing. At least, not yet. And if I'd have had a bucket of water handy I would have washed my hands of the whole business.

'Ee aye adio, I don't fucking think so,' Gaz trilled. 'I'm going back tonight with Darren. Get meself a few more handfuls.'

I grabbed his T-shirt and hauled him off the fence. 'Oh no you're bloody well not,' I hissed in his filthy face.

'YOU are going to do exactly as I tell you.'

Gaz looked startled, momentarily afraid.

'Breathe a word of this to anyone or go near that garage again and I'll be on the phone to your family before you know where you are. Got it?'

My gamble paid off. He looked terrified.

'All right, all right. But I'm keeping what I've got.'

I nodded. It seemed like a good enough compromise. For the moment.

'Now what?' he asked.

I thought about it. 'We're keeping this to ourselves. Just the three of us –'

'Four of us,' Gaz corrected me.

'Until we decide what to do. And get that film to Janice as fast as you can.' I pointed to the camera. 'You never know what else is on it. And where is the Caddy? And Darren?'

'He'll be home by now. I'll ring him. Sort sommat out,' Gaz said, cheerful again. 'Don't panic, I'll get Janice to give you a bell.' He reached into his various pockets and pulled out an assortment of banknotes, which he counted as quickly as any Barclays teller. 'Five hundred and seventy quid! Just like that.' He snapped his fingers for emphasis. 'Anyway, I'm off home, I've got to get tea ready.'

I reeled with the idea of Gaz as a New Man. He set off down the path, whirling the camera strap over his head.

'You coming?' he asked.

'Jesus, Letty! You stink,' were AnnaMaria's opening words when I finally staggered over the threshold of the farm.

Trance music filled the house and I headed for the

kettle before I lost the will to live. 'Anyway,' I said guiltily avoiding questions or confrontations, 'you're home early. And where's Liam?' I was amazed I could hold anything like a normal conversation.

'If you call six o'clock early,' AnnaMaria muttered as she flung open the cooker door. 'And Liam's at Anne's for the night. I'm sure I told you. Oh, and your mum rang. Twice. She's gone to Ireland with Harry. She said she needed a break. She'll ring when she gets back.' She turned to me as a waft of baked potatoes filled the kitchen.

'You look like you've seen a ghost,' she observed flatly. 'And Letty, for Christ's sake,' she added in alarm. 'You're bleeding! Look at your elbows.'

I glanced down. 'It's stopped,' I said lamely.

'What sort of explanation is that?' she asked, suddenly angry.

'I fell.'

'What off? A train?'

I shrugged, feeling guilty again. 'You don't want to know.'

'It's that fucking Janice, isn't it? I saw you going off with her *and* you were heading in the same direction as those two hooligans. I saw them in the Cadillac earlier. Want to tell me what's going on?' She stared at me. Her hands were balled into fists and thick cords of muscle stood out on her bare arms.

'It's . . .'

AnnaMaria glared.

' . . . too complicated,' I finished, pathetically.

'Well, when it gets *uncomplicated* perhaps you'd like to share it. With me preferably. I don't want to hear it second hand.' And with that she turned abruptly and went back to the oven. I could see she was livid, but there was nothing I could do about it.

170

Instead I stated the obvious, 'I'm late,' and headed for the backyard and the starving chickens beyond.

'I've fed the birds,' AnnaMaria said angrily. 'Thank you is acceptable and she's on the side porch, if you're interested. She's been here ages.'

Despite *everything* my groin did a flip-flop of interest and I turned tail and headed for the porch.

'Letty,' AnnaMaria hissed. 'I know you haven't dated for a while but a wash before you go out is usual, I think. You can tell me why you need one so badly later.' She had a point.

I tried ringing AnnaMaria's least favourite person from the upstairs phone. There was no reply from the landline or her mobile, so I left a brief message on her voice mail. I toyed with the idea of ringing WPC Emma Auckland but thought better of it. I'd been the one helping to break and enter. If mud was going to fly, a lot of it was coming my way.

As an almost last resort I rang Julia but she was out somewhere. The first time ever that I'd known her to be unreachable. Sylvia Buckham didn't even come into the equation. I had all sorts of questions and suspicions and possibly only one person to share them with.

I had a quick shower, flayed my already flayed skin with a flannel and slapped antiseptic ointment on my cuts and grazes. My fingers, healing now, were left unbound. I chucked on clean but haphazardly ironed clothes. I chose a long-sleeved Calvin Klein top. I didn't want our conversation to start with 'What the hell happened to you?'

Sarah was leaning over the railing surrounding the porch, and staring into the farmyard beyond. She looked gorgeous and my horrendous afternoon was swept away as I took a stolen moment to spy on her.

Her clothes were fastidiously ironed. A perfect crease ran down the arms of her white silk shirt and her loose-fitting black linen trousers looked brand new.

My heart swelled in the hope that all this effort was just for me.

'Anything worth seeing?' I asked after a moment or two. She started in surprise and looked over her shoulder.

'Hiya,' she said and smiled, looking me up and down, with approval, I thought. 'Nice outfit,' she confirmed.

She pushed herself away from the railings and, still smiling, reached for my hand, pulled me to her and kissed me on the mouth. I kissed her back with an urgency that shook me. Being scared to death gives you an appetite for a lot of things, and this was one of them.

I thought about postponing our meal as I held Sarah, squeezed her, grabbed her backside with both hands. Her head came up and she looked at me, surprised and pleased. Perhaps I could ask AnnaMaria to make herself scarce. Bad idea – I wasn't her favourite person at the moment. And I'd not eaten since . . . God! I couldn't remember when, or what come to that. And then my stomach grumbled, loud and insistent.

'I think your stomach is trying to tell me something.' Sarah pulled away, laughing. 'Come on, you lovely, hungry beast, let's get you fed. Everything else can wait.'

She took my hand and led me to her car.

Chapter 24

I didn't let the day's events encroach. I refused to even consider them. If a moment presented itself I would tell Sarah the details of my strange afternoon. But not yet.

Sarah drove mostly one-handed, letting go of my thigh only when the engine informed her she really had to change gear. The little Nissan Micra was a doddle to drive anyway.

I kept my hand pressed against hers and thigh stroking changed to fondling, fondling to kneading. We didn't say much, we didn't need to. I could only think about the here and now or, if I let myself, how Sarah would cope in the back seats. I even took a quick glimpse to see if there would be room. I decided we could make room.

'Pull down here,' I said as we skirted Huddersfield Avenue. I knew a side road. A rarely used side road.

'Isn't Langton that –?'

'Shut up Sarah,' I said, smiling. 'And just follow my instructions.' She did.

Eventually we hit the café bar in Langton, a little later than planned, admittedly.

As the home of ex-lover Anne, I'd nearly declined the venue. But in a *Bridget Jones* moment of utter shallowness I had decided that being seen with another woman would be no bad thing. Even in Langton.

Despite the near starvation of an hour ago I thought I'd be unable to order coffee, much less a full meal. But in the end, suspecting everything would taste the same, I'd gone for stuffed tomatoes and Greek salad and a bottle of cheap white Cava that I drank like fizzy pop. Sarah had pasta and just a small glass of wine. All we needed was Nana Mouskouri, a couple of dozen scrawny cats and fading overhead awnings to recreate that Mediterranean ambience.

Talk was lanquid; after-sex conversation. Sarah didn't look quite so pristine any more. Her dark hair was stuck up at all angles and she'd buttoned her blouse the wrong way. I didn't tell her. If she moved a certain way I got a shot of her cleavage.

We sat opposite each other. She'd slipped her shoes off, her toes kept trying to climb under the cuff of my trousers. I was delirious with sex, with hunger, with the weirdness of the day. But I was *alive*. And I felt it. Every nerve, every fibre had its own song. I finally felt *awake* again.

Unfortunately, the arrival of pudding coincided with the appearance of Amy, dining alone.

Sarah's attitude couldn't have changed any more dramatically if Hannibal Lecter had walked in clutching a bottle of Chianti.

The café wasn't crowded and though the waiter indicated a window seat, Amy took a table directly behind ours. It was a deliberate move. Why she didn't simply sprinkle ground glass in our food was anybody's guess. Judging by Sarah's reaction, she would have preferred the glass.

174

We really tried not to let her spoil things, we really did, but it didn't work. Sarah slipped her shoes back on and shrugged.

'Well, at least I can eat normally now,' I said quietly across the table.

Sarah giggled and reached for her spoon. 'So, what else have you been up to today?' she asked.

'Apart from sex with you?' I whispered. God, that wine was stronger than I thought. Sarah laughed. She had her back to Amy and was out of her line of vision, perhaps she'd put her out of her mind too. 'You must have done something else,' she said. 'Mountain biking? Skateboarding? Wrestling chickens perhaps?'

I looked at her. 'What?'

She leaned over. 'The elbows,' she said and pointed at her own. 'You've lost a yard of skin somewhere.'

I'd forgotten that she'd seen me more or less naked since my adventures at Tyre and Tread.

'You wouldn't believe me if I told you,' I said, not, I hoped, too coyly.

'Try me.' She smirked. Despite Amy, sexual banter was back on the agenda.

I ordered coffee as the waiter came within earshot. I pushed my glass to one side. 'I've had enough,' I explained to Sarah. 'Any more wine and I'll have you across the table.'

She smiled. She didn't look as though she'd raise too many objections. The waiter might though. And Miss Anal Amy certainly would.

Anal Amy. It had a certain ring to it.

'So, what else have you been up to today?' she insisted. She placed her spoon and fork haphazardly on her plate and sat back, rummaging in her pocket for her cigarettes. I noticed that Amy, directly behind her, sat back too. One wayward elbow and ribs would crack.

'Well, it wasn't my usual day, I must admit,' I said and my weird afternoon came flooding back.

She lit her cigarette, a Marlboro Light, not her customary roll-up, and stared at me over the rush of smoke.

'I saw you earlier with that journalist, Janice is she called?' Sarah said quietly so only I could hear. She tapped ash into a stainless steel ashtray.

'I didn't know you'd met,' I said and reached across the table for her hand. The waiter did a double take on his way past. Sarah grinned conspiratorially.

'She tried to get the lowdown on Chris at the Health Club. Came wandering into the kitchen. Is she always such a nosy cow?'

I laughed. 'You don't know the half of it. I bet Chris didn't like the tables being turned, did she?' I said, remembering that CFC's owner had already delved into the background of all and sundry.

'That's putting it mildly.' Sarah stubbed out her cigarette and gripped my hand with both of hers. She leaned across the table as I prepared to launch into my story, but then her mobile rang.

Sarah's reaction when she knocked off the *Popeye* theme tune and muttered 'Hello' was a shock. She stood up suddenly and I heard an incredulous 'What?' Her chair crashed backwards catching Amy's elbow and her handbag went crashing to the floor. I had a quick glance at our fellow diner. A cloud of anger flushed Amy's cheeks. She wiped her mouth with her napkin, pushing a barely touched coffee cup to one side. The other diners looked around briefly though they soon went back to their meals when they saw the look of alarm on Sarah's face.

She turned away from me and I didn't catch any other part of her conversation. Eventually she slipped the phone back into her pocket.

She made no attempt to pick up her chair and instead, agitated, grabbed her car keys from the table.

'Look, I'm really sorry about this but I've got to go. Do you mind paying?' she asked quietly. She took my hand and squeezed my fingers tenderly. 'I've only got plastic and I can't wait. You'll be okay getting home? I'm needed,' she muttered, stepping between Amy's table and its occupant's visual line of fire.

Sarah faced me, an odd imploring expression on her face. She frowned, put her fingers to her mouth in a shushing motion and tapped her chest. Fingers flashed against her T-shirt, a hooked finger here, the stroke of a thumb against a palm there. Then she turned tail, squeezed past Amy – who was still grappling for the contents of her bag – and was gone.

Now I might be crap at languages but I knew enough to recognise deaf signing when I saw it.

I had no idea what she'd said, mind, but I knew someone who would. I was going to do something that I swore I would never do.

I was going to see Anne.

Chapter 25

Langton is a picturesque place, less of a working village than Calderton, and Anne's cottage fitted the mould perfectly.

I'd never visited her new home though I knew exactly where it was. Call me obsessional, but I'd taken the time to find out the name and location of her love nest. If AnnaMaria hadn't stopped me I would probably have investigated the exact dimensions of its rooms.

So Little Lane Cottage, down the road from Little Lane Farm and Little Lane Nursery (the floral kind), wasn't such a shock when I did finally get to see it. Set back from the bumpy road, the cottage with its small wooden porch and rose-filled front garden would, once upon a time, have filled me with the urge to petrol bomb it.

A 'For Sale' sign had been erected in the garden. 'Sold' was nailed across it, half obscuring the wood. Anne's move to London was definite after all, then.

Lights shone throughout the house and I could see straight into the front room. A tall figure picked up a smaller one and hoisted him onto a shoulder. No prizes for spotting Anne and Liam in bonding process.

I kicked the front gate and, I admit, took some

pleasure as it flew open and decapitated a couple of Princess Margaret roses.

A security light clicked on as I quickly marched down the path, not giving myself time to change my mind. The door opened before I had chance to knock.

Debbie Jones, Anne's agent and lover, stood on the threshold stuffing her fat face with a doorstop of toast. I took a deep breath. Although I really didn't give a shit any more, thinking these ungracious thoughts was no way to start.

'Well,' she said. 'Letty.'

'Last time I checked,' I remarked before I could stop myself.

Debbie looked me up and down and managed not to sneer. She made no move to let me in. Instead, she called over her shoulder, 'Anne, for you.' She then closed, but didn't slam, the door in my face.

'Letty,' Liam shrieked when the door opened again. He struggled out of Anne's arms and threw himself at my legs. Bless him.

'Letty?' Anne said.

Fairly unanimous verdict on my identity, then.

'Do you want to come in?' she asked.

If I did, I would finally get a look at those room dimensions but I declined the offer. I swallowed, feeling foolish. 'I'm after a favour,' I began, and even after all this time her suddenly guarded look made me sad.

I retrieved the napkin from my back pocket and held it aloft, away from Liam's clutching fingers. 'You know signing, don't you?' I asked into the awkward silence.

Anne blinked. 'Deaf signing?' she asked, puzzled.

I nodded. 'Do you know what these mean?'

Anyone else would have asked for more information, more details, but we had been so close, such soul mates for so long that I knew she would be able to fathom out my sketches, as rough as they were.

'I need more light,' she said finally. 'And my reading glasses,' she admitted with a small laugh. 'Please come in, Letty. You *are* welcome here.'

As welcome as a toenail in a takeaway pizza. But I went in, Liam on my heels.

Debbie's presence was all over the place. Photos; hers and hers images everywhere. The woman herself clutched at Liam and steered him towards the stairs, bedroom bound. The little boy, already dressed in pyjamas, was too knackered to complain and he waved a silent goodbye at me as Debbie led him from the room.

I took a seat on the edge of a too-soft settee. I felt as though the big cream cushions would swallow me without trace. Anne, an Anne I didn't really know, sat at her desk in one corner of the knocked through dining room, donned her glasses and scanned the images on the napkin. After a moment the glasses came off and she looked at me with a frown.

'Want to give me any background?' she asked. 'Anything to do with your accident? I heard it was a nasty one.'

I shook my head at the woman that had once shared my life and any thoughts, hopes and wishes I may ever have had.

She sighed and put her glasses on again.

'This is simple. It's a warning.' She paused to look at me over her rims. 'It says: "She's listening, watching, following. Meet me. Farm. One hour." Anne paused. 'And a bit here I'm not sure about. "Help me", at a guess, if your drawings are accurate.' She crossed her slim legs and scraped hair behind an ear. Anne was ten years older than me but tonight she looked ten years younger. Mind you, I could have given Methuselah a run for his money at the moment.

'Thanks,' I said and got up.

Debbie appeared at the door. 'Liam wants a story, but not from me,' she said with a smile. If Anne seemed young, Debbie looked as though she'd just slipped out of her school uniform.

I headed for the door, Anne right behind me.

'Are you sure you're all right?' she asked. 'I wish you'd keep in touch,' she added.

I resisted a reply, waved goodbye and took off down the path, relieved to be out of the house and away from them both.

Well, at least I now knew what Sarah had said though I had no idea what she *meant*.

Who was following? Amy?

And why? A nasty possibility gripped me. Did someone know of my afternoon's activities? Someone other than Liz? Had she seen me? Followed me? I glanced around. Had Gaz blabbed to somebody? How trustworthy were the two boys? I should have called Emma, I finally admitted to myself. The streets were completely deserted. The sprinkling of houses were mostly in darkness, an odd bedroom light shining out – early to retire, folks in these parts.

I checked my watch. Less than half an hour left to Sarah's strange deadline and a three-mile walk ahead. Shame I didn't think to ask Anne for a lift. Perhaps as well. No chance of a taxi. Not in Langton midweek. Not in Langton, full stop.

I set off down the road. The sun hadn't set and was still a bright presence on the horizon. No need for street lights – as thin on the ground as taxis – just yet.

I'd covered about a mile and a half and there was no
way I was going to get to the farm within the allotted
time. Dusk had settled at last and the path before me
stretched ever into darkness. This was spooky if familiar
territory. I trudged on.

An owl hooted somewhere and at one horrible moment,
just as my imagining had taken on Poe-like qualities, a fox
skittered ahead of me to disappear into the thick bushes
alongside the path. My heart skittered too and my dinner
was jammed somewhere between my foodpipe and
stomach. In years to come, I reckoned, I would be able to
pinpoint the exact time my ulcer was born.

In the distance, not so very far behind me, I heard the
growl of a powerful car. It was heading in my direction.
I considered taking cover with the fox but pulled myself
together. This was the short road stretching between
Langton and Calderton. Not some Project in the Bronx.
I turned round and stuck my thumb out and was
rewarded with blinding full beams.

The car shrieked past me, sending gravel into the air.
Brake lights appeared. Then small but piercing white
lights, and the big car sped towards me, faster than
anyone should ever reverse.

I didn't have chance to jump out of the way, every
muscle in my body had seized, but the car stopped
inches from my toes.

A face peered out. 'I've been looking for you all over
the goddamned place. Letty, get in the car. Now!'

'I'm not putting up with this crap!' Christine Crozier
bellowed as she slammed the Ford Senator into drive
and ground her foot on the accelerator.

Mach two distorted my face as we tore down the

road. I didn't get chance to say anything to the woman or ask her what she meant. I'd got in the car as commanded, amazed to see Chris, never mind hear that she'd been looking for me.

I saw the Calderton traffic lights over the horizon, they were just turning red. Chris floored the accelerator.

'Chris,' I warned.

She ignored me and as we hit a depression in the road the car bellyflopped briefly and all four wheels left the tarmac. We came down with a bang and images of my brush with death on the outskirts of Scotland came screaming back into my mind.

'*Chris!*'

The lights changed to red and orange and we skipped through them at an incredibly illegal sixty-five miles an hour.

Calderton, like Langton, was deserted though I noticed lights blazing and someone pottering about in Mrs Buckham's shop as we shot past. In seconds we were through the village and amazingly no one had been killed.

'Chris, you're going to have to stop,' I said as forcefully as I could. 'I'm going to be sick.'

We screeched to a halt and I managed to undo the seatbelt and swing open the door before my lovely meal at the café was deposited on the roadside.

I slumped back in my seat.

'Come on, honey. Get that belt fastened,' Chris said, agitated. Her blonde hair was all over the place, bits of hay clung to her fringe, muck and dust were smeared all over her.

'No,' I gasped. 'Not until you tell me ...' I petered out. She could guess the rest of the sentence.

'Okay.' She sighed and reluctantly yanked on the handbrake. 'It's Sarah. I think she's in trouble.'

Chapter 26

'How much do you know about her? I mean, really know?' Christine began.

'Enough,' I said defensively. I suddenly had to remind myself that I wasn't speaking to my mother. 'She used to live around here. She's travelled a bit. Learned her trade in some sort of institution where she worked,' I said, recalling our conversations. 'Why am I telling you all this?' I asked. 'You probably know a damn sight more than I do. And how can she be in trouble? What sort of trouble? I only left her an hour ago.' I hadn't forgotten her signed message, of course, though somehow I didn't want to share it with her employer.

Christine rested her foot on the accelerator and the engine roared. She was itching to get going. She turned to me, smiling.

'She has travelled. That's true. And she did learn to cook in an institution, and in a sense I suppose, honey, you could say she worked there.'

I twisted towards her and the leather seat creaked beneath me. 'Chris, please. No riddles. I've had a hell of a day.'

'Yes,' she said quietly. 'I've heard. Anyway, look, here's

the deal. Sarah Flowers is an ex-con.'

By sheer strength of will, I kept my face expressionless. 'Go on,' I said, trying to keep the tremor of shock out of my voice. How many surprises could I cope with in one day? I tried to deal logically with this unexpected image of my new lover. She was an ex-con? Who was I to judge her anyway?

'You didn't know?' Chris asked.

I shook my head. I was too stunned to speak again.

For reasons best known to herself, she laughed and lightly slapped the steering wheel.

'Well, goddamn. She did keep her mouth shut after all. I didn't think she'd be able to resist telling you,' she muttered to herself. 'Sit back,' she went on. 'I'll explain on the way.'

She touched the accelerator again and nervously I gripped the seat.

'She was in Styal with Lorna Thompson, though I believe she already knew her.' Chris paused, waiting for a reaction. 'I think I'm right in saying you've heard of her.'

I nodded and gazed out of the window. A variety of emotions greeted the news. None of them pleasant. I was shocked, and I struggled with disbelief. I didn't want to trust Chris's word, despite her intimate knowledge of all my friends and aquaintances. And lovers.

The gaudy lights of CFC Health Club suddenly appeared on the horizon. I sighed. 'I suppose we'll be relatives of a sort when Mum gets married. Her fiancé is Lorna's –'

'Yeah, I know all that,' Chris drawled. 'I've had you checked out,' she reminded me. 'Well, Sarah and Lorna sought each other out, if you get my meaning.'

'So why are you telling me this? Religious crap has

finally made you judge and executioner, has it?' I snapped angrily. Who the hell did she think she was?

'You'll see,' Chris said quietly. The little Texan woman began to slow the car to swing it right onto a side road. We weren't going to the farm after all. I tensed. Rage suddenly made way for nervousness.

'Chris, where are we going?' I asked.

'Christ, woman, you've still not guessed. I was led to believe you were intelligent.'

'What the fuck are you on about now?'

Something cold, thin and hard was suddenly whipped over my head and a tight band of wire closed over my throat.

'Shut the fuck up and let the good lady tell the *story*,' a man's voice suggested from the back seat. A man I hadn't even realised was in the back of the car.

I swallowed, barely, and gave one painful and terrified nod.

'You know a boy named Gaz?' Chris asked conversationally. Our speed had slowed to about twenty miles an hour, which was both a good thing and a bad thing. Good, because we were less likely to crash and bad because, one way or another, I had an awful feeling I was about to exit the car.

I nodded quickly, appeasingly.

'Of course she does. She's been with the little fuck all day,' the mystery man said. The garotte tightened. I leaned back against the seat to take the pressure off.

'What do you want?' I managed. My voice had turned into some terror-filled, squeakily inept thing. 'Please,' I gasped. 'Don't.'

'Oh, *please, don't*,' the man mimicked.

'So where is he?' Chris asked.

The wire was bitting into my neck. 'I don't know,' I whispered. Tears began to roll down my face. I didn't care what speed the car was going now, the cold hard piece of metal was all I could think about.

I reached up to claw at my neck, felt blood. The world swam away from me.

'Ease up, Lee,' Chris suggested. 'No goddamn good if she's dead, boy.'

The pressure lifted slightly. I managed to push a couple of fingers between my neck and the wire.

Lee laughed. It was the most hideous sound I'd ever heard. He gave a playful little tug and I thought my finger tops were going to be sliced off. I wriggled them away and the pressure was back on my neck. The pain, like his laughter, was hideous.

'We know where he lives,' Chris went on as though this were the most normal of conversations. 'But he ain't there either.' The more Chris spoke, the more pronounced her Texan accent became.

'Why do you want him?' I squeaked as Lee tugged the wire just a tiny fraction tighter.

'You're more stupid than we thought.' Lee giggled. 'If she's the most intelligent of the lot, I'd hate to meet the dumbest.'

'*Tyre place*?' he went on playfully. Another tug. '*Money? Ring any bells*?' The playful tone vanished. 'Any' – tug – 'idea' – tug – 'where?'

The world swam again. I was seconds from blackout. Finally I had an idea. As painful as it was, I managed one small nod. Lee released the wire and my head fell forward. Gasping, eyes full of tears and with blood trickling down my neck, I whispered, 'Got a mobile?'

Chapter 27

Lee dangled the garotte in front of my face. 'No tricks, now.'

I juggled the mobile phone and wiped blood from my hands down my jeans. Chris had pulled the car over onto the deserted side road. She sighed. 'Too messy all this,' she grumbled. 'Get on with it.' I took a deep breath, muttered a quick prayer to any gods listening, well any god except Chris Crozier's, and dialled.

Anne answered the phone on the eighth ring, just as I was about to give up. My next choice would have to be Julia. But that was the last resort.

'Hiya. Mrs Buckham,' I said cheerfully, croakily. 'It's Letty here. I wondered if you could do me a favour.' My captors were listening in but fortunately Anne's pause was so brief only I noticed.

'Hello, Letty. Are you okay?'

'Yes, yes.' My voice was threatening to give out. 'I wondered,' I went on with a squeak. I tried to clear my throat but the pain was dizzying, powerfully distracting. 'I wondered if you could give me Gaz's mobile number.'

That pause again. I felt Lee stiffen and one long arm came round the back of the headrest to lay gently across my breasts. I tried hard not to throw up, suddenly glad I had done so earlier.

'Gaz?' Anne queried. I could imagine her bewilderment.

'Yes, Gaz. You know him. Dreadlocks. I need him for...'What? Why did I need him? 'To help on the farm. Tomorrow. But I've got to sort it out. Today. Tonight. The number is under "E", his surname. Next to Em. You know Em. She works at the station,' I rambled on, my vocal cords gaining a little strength. Would Anne ever get the hint?

'Oh yes, I've got it,' Anne said, all nervous curiosity. 'Shall I ring? Or do you want to do it?'

'Just give me the number,' I croaked.

Anne hesitated again but reeled off the digits, which I repeated one by one for Lee to jot down.

'Thanks, Sylvia,' I whispered almost inaudibly into the phone. 'Give my –'

The phone was snatched from my hand.

'Nice try,' Lee giggled again. 'Sylvia, eh?' he whispered into my ear as Chris punched numbers. 'Bit foxy, eh? Another fucking closet case?'

Even amid all this I had to stifle a hysterical giggle. Sylvia Buckham as a foxy chick? It was a thought you could die with.

My hysteria evaporated. Chris passed me the phone. But my call to WPC Emma Auckland remained unanswered.

Chris Crozier tapped her fingers on the steering wheel in time to some little tune playing over and over in her head.

Lee's arm was draped across me again and his unpleasantly hot breath belched at the back of my neck.

His presence, the threat of violence both actual and imagined, made me feel helpless. A victim. A wimp.

Tears were close again. Only by imagining myself anywhere but in this place, in this car, with these people, did I keep them at bay.

The Ford's engine was still running, and heat filled the cab. Sweat dripped from Lee's face onto my neck and my skin crawled.

Chris turned to me and I sank further into the leather seats.

'Tell me what you were planning,' she ordered. She rested her chin on her hand and smiled. 'And then tell me how you thought you were going to get away with it.'

Lee's grip tightened. 'You can manage that, can't you?' he asked pleasantly. He placed the piece of wire across my chest. I nodded my head, and told them what I knew.

Chris kept shaking her head the whole time I talked. She even laughed once or twice. I wanted to laugh too, but thought if I started, I'd never stop.

She gazed out of the window to a horizon bathed in complete darkness.

'No, no, no!' Chris said and she grabbed my T-shirt. Lee released his grip and sat back in his seat. I could smell Chris's perfume. Some flowery, pleasant aroma, incongruous in the circumstances. But maybe not. Maybe more like roses on a grave.

'You expect me to believe this bullshit? You were in the garage because you thought there was a *funding* con going on? And you left the money where it was? Oh please. Get real, honey. Just tell me where you moved it. That's all I'm asking. The Mercs are somewhere. It's in your interest' – she paused and added quietly – 'and in your *girlfriend's* interest to tell me where it's stashed.

Don't make me spell it out, Letty. We'd just be wasting our time.'

'Does Amy know about this?' I choked out a sudden thought.

'Amy? Jesus no!' Lee said. 'Fucking cocksucker.'

'Lee!' Chris exploded. 'Keep your mouth shut if that's the best you can do.' She pushed her fist into my chest. '*I haven't got the time for this.* Where's the money? Just tell me where the goddamn *money* is.'

'I've told you,' I whispered. 'At the garage. In the blankets. I saw it. Today. With my own eyes.' I pleaded with her to understand, but she didn't relinquish her grip on my T-shirt.

'Do you know how much money we're talking about here? Huh?'

I shook my head. I felt as though my brain were rattling around in there. 'I don't know anything about it.'

Lee laughed. 'Jesus!' He pounded the back of the seat with his fist. I cringed as he breathed into my ear. 'Lorna Thompson and her robbery. Fill in the gaps yourself.' And with those words things began to slip into place.

'Twelve a half million pounds. That's over *twenty-five million dollars*.' Chris's words hung unchallenged in the air. 'Even a cut of that would finally get the old man off my back. Do you know how sick I am of leaning on him? I don't own a thing! I haven't got a cent to my name. I'm just a manager for him. His own daughter. A manager. Damn.' She pushed me away and wiped a hand across her frustrated face. Suddenly she dropped the car into gear and floored the accelerator.

'How did you know about the money?' I asked wildly. My voice gained a little more strength – I needed them to think I was still important, still useful. I had to remind Chris I was there.

191

'Oh, how in hell do you think?' Lee taunted from the back seat. 'Do you think your girlfriend couldn't put a truckload of money to good use? Pillow talk,' he said and giggled at his own peculiarly old-fashioned turn of phrase. 'Imagine how much planning you can do in a prison. There's fuck all else to do. I should know, I've been there,' he said ominously. 'All that money waiting. Four years buried under a shitload of old floorboards. But there were others after it, and Lorna needed a bit of a helping hand to make her break. It ain't the sort of thing you can do alone.' He leaned forward and wrapped his big arms around my chest, kissed me wetly on the cheek. He tittered as I pulled away violently, disgusted. 'And when Sarah went to work for Mr Crozier, well, she soon found out that his daughter had the special touch. And, for a price, that inside knowledge.' He turned to look admiringly at his boss. 'The rest of the team were all lining up to have a shot at it too. But they lucked out.' A pause to let that sink in. 'And Sarah. The lovely Sarah. It seems to me she used and abused you.' He laughed and a spray of saliva hit my neck. Letting me go, he clapped his hands together joyfully.

I turned in my seat so suddenly there was nothing either of them could do. 'Did you no bloody good though, did it?' I spat at him. My voice went from croak to shout and back to croak again. His hair, the brush scrub of militia, was shiny with sweat and the dark sharp eyes beneath it narrowed dangerously. 'You've still not got the money, have you, you fucking dickhead?'

The punch in the head was expected, though the source was a bit of a shock. Chris's fist crunched into my temple and the world spun. I could hear shouting, the sounds of wheels spinning against loose soil as Chris

192

grappled with the wheel; could vaguely feel a hand in my hair. I struggled, grabbed the door handle and yanked it open. The blast of cool night air as the passenger door swung wide was sobering, terrifying. I got a glimpse of tarmac speeding by as full-beamed lights from a car close behind suddenly lit up the road. The black surface reached up to claim me; a brief but intense burning sensation and then a quiet, soft drifting into space.

Chapter 28

I dreamed I was by a fire. I could smell smoke, hear fireworks in the background. Children's voices over the beat of music. Loud music. Insistent rap. Heavy stuff, more Puff Daddy than Will Smith. How did I know this? What did I know about rap? Only what I was hearing now. The pros and cons of East Coast versus West Coast that had raged through the nineties.

I tried to get back to the peaceful fire, the sparklers and Catherine wheels but Puff Daddy drew me upwards.

I opened an eye and saw the back of a car seat. A full seat in cream, no partition or split, just a solid bank of leather. I had a single moment's terror that was so clear, so utterly, horribly real that a scream was out of my throat before I could stop it.

Gaz popped his head over the back of the seat.

'Letty, my man!' he said in delight. A spliff, almost as thick as his skinny forearm, was shoved in my face. 'Come on,' he said. 'If anybody needs it, you do.'

Under teenage pressure I inhaled a couple of times – distant days of clubbing revisited – before the tobacco caught in my throat. I coughed and struggled to a sitting position. I waited for excruciating pain but felt instead intermittent and vague aches down my right side. A bandage was wound tightly round my forearm and my neck was oily with what smelled like Germoline.

'Have we been to the hospital?' I asked in a small uneasy voice.

'Nah,' Gaz said. 'Darren did that. He's been on a course. He reckoned you'd come round in a bit. We picked you up out of the ditch. We'd been following that mad cow for ages. She never even noticed.' He paused for a toke on his spliff. 'You had a nice soft landing. Once you'd bounced off the tarmac, like.'

'How did you . . . ?'

'That lass you used to shag,' Darren said from behind the steering wheel of the Cadillac. 'She rang Gaz. Said she got this really weird phone call from you asking for him. Got all mixed up about that copper. Dead confused she was. Tried to get hold of the local plod, but there's been some big crash on the M62. Lorry turned over or summat, cars backed up for miles. The local constabulary' – he said this with great care – 'are otherwise engaged. So she asked us to have a scout round. Lucky for you.' Darren took the spliff from Gaz's hand. I looked out of the window, once again scared for my life on this endless day, but we were trundling down one of Calderton's back roads at about fifteen miles an hour. No danger there.

'And she didn't think to ring 999?'

Gaz shrugged. 'Thought that might be a bit . . .'

'Dramatic.' Darren finished the sentence with a giggle.

Gaz leaned over the back of the seat again. His head was plumed in smoke. He waved a hand in front of his face to get a better look at me.

'You're not gonna chuck up, are you?' he asked. That

was twice he'd shown concern about my stomach.

'No.'

'Good, 'cause Darren's dad would go mad.'

'What happened to yer neck?' Darren asked.

'Somebody tried to strangle me with a wire.'

'Garotte!' the boys chorused. 'Cool.'

'Who?' Gaz asked.

'Why?' Darren echoed.

I sighed and swallowed with some difficulty. 'That American woman you've been following.'

'*She* tried to strangle ya? Wow,' Darren exclaimed.

I didn't bother trying to explain the intricacies. My throat couldn't take it. 'She's after that money. The blanket money.'

Gaz looked at Darren and giggled. Darren, returning the look, laughed with him and then took for ever to turn his attention back to the road. The road was straight, the car perfectly aligned and he needed to adjust his steering only a minimal amount.

'What's funny?' I asked.

'She'll never find it,' Gaz stated.

'Why?'

''Cause we've got it, that's why.'

'Give me that spliff,' I ordered. 'I need it.'

'It's where?' I asked incredulously.

'In the boot,' the boys chorused again. They were stoned best mates: speaking in unison, finishing each other's sentences. 'THE CADDY'S BOOT,' they sang and fell about with laughter. Our speed slowed to ten miles an hour.

'You're driving around with it?' I gasped. 'All of it?'

'Well, some of it.' Gaz wiped his eyes. 'We went back to the tyre place earlier tonight. 'Course I thought it would've all been shifted and sure enough, most of it had. One of the vans were gone. But we managed to get our hands on a bit more dosh, didn't we, Darren?' Gaz looked admiringly at Darren. There'd been some subtle power shift here. 'So we broke in again, and waited till there was a break in the *activity.*'

'Yeah, lots of *activity,*' Darren snorted mysteriously. 'That redhead were there.'

'Liz.' A huge beacon illuminated my thoughts, the proverbial lightbulb in my head came on, and I made a drug-induced connection.

For Liz read Lorna.

'Anybody else?' I asked, my voice catching. Memories burned in my mind.

'Some other bird in a uniform. Didn't know her though. Little, fat, short dark hair.'

'Sarah,' I muttered.

'And that posh one. Megan. Solicitor or summat,' Darren said.

'Megan? Are you sure?'

'Yep.' Gaz took up the story as his friend concentrated on driving. We began to pick up speed, but only very slightly. 'Three of 'em. Took a while to finish loadin' them blankets. I suppose they went back for the rest.' Gaz wound down his window and flicked the remains of the joint out into the night. I saw sparks fly briefly before the dark swallowed it up.

'Does Janice know any of this?' I asked.

'Nah, couldn't find her,' Darren said.

'Only 'cause you never looked,' Gaz pointed out with a snort of laughter.

'She would have only gone to the cops, once she'd got her *story,*' Darren sneered. 'You know what reporters are like. Said she'd give us fifty quid. Hah, only got a tenner out of her. Cost more than that for the petrol,' he droned on.

'So what now?' I asked.

'Dunno. D'ya want to look at the garage, though there's nowt there?'

'Have you got a phone?' I asked.

'Yeah, but the batteries have just packed in. Forgot to charge them last night.'

'Well, let's head back to my place, plan our next move, okay? I'll call the police, 999 this time, from there.'

'I'll roll another joint then,' Gaz decided. 'Just got time to smoke it.'

Chapter 29

My farm was in darkness – clearly AnnaMaria had gone out – unlike CFC Health Club which blazed with lights. I thought with horror of my experiences with the manager of the club. But I hoped she'd be long gone. Sadly, so would Sarah and I felt a suprising and painful tug of regret. Whatever trouble she was in, well, I couldn't help her now.

I wondered for a moment how the paying guests were getting along on this particular rudderless ship. They'd be screaming for their tea by now, I shouldn't wonder.

'I'll go the back way, it's quicker,' Darren said and before I could stop him he was steering the unwieldy piece of Americana towards the road that I'd previously shared with my neighbour.

'It's closed off,' I began, but we were facing the high wooden gate before I could finish my sentence.

'Shit, I'll have to turn around,' Darren said and he slammed the car into reverse.

'I'm keeping the money, y'know,' Gaz said insistently, loudly.

'Yeah, we've worked hard for this dosh,' Darren commented. 'If you think we're just handing it back you've got . . . ' He trailed off.

Above the bantering, Darren had failed to notice the gate in front of us opening.'

'Frig,' he said in a voice stripped of any false bravado. This was a young boy's voice, whose audible hitch of fear was enough to silence us all.

Halifax Tyre and Tread
The nameplate above the door hung at right angles, soft night breezes causing it to rock gently against the prefabricated framework.

The garage was completely in darkness except for a dim light shining beneath the door. Lee – hostage taker for the evening – dragged the three of us out of the car onto the track in front of the garage.

We leaned against each other; safety in numbers, anonymity in a group. Ancient herding, animal instincts bound the three of us together. We were terror stricken, our hands immobilised by wire.

Lee tapped on the metal door with the butt of a mean-looking gun. I gulped, none too pleased that he'd come prepared. 'It's me,' he yelled. He pushed a key into the lock and the door swung open.

Lee shoved me in first and, with my hands tightly secured behind my back, I stumbled across the threshold. Gaz and Darren, similarly unbalanced, crashed into me. We landed in a heap on the floor.

I looked around, trying to get my bearings.

Christine Crozier sat on the edge of a work-bench, short but muscular legs hanging over the side. Facing her was Sarah, dark hair a mess around her bruised and swollen face. Her shirt was ripped open and bruising pitted her skin. Blood dripped steadily from a cut above her top lip. She was bound to an old tractor tyre and her head lolled to one side.

'Sarah? Oh my God,' I croaked and she looked up groggily at the sound of her name. One eye managed to focus on me before her head fell forward again.

There was no one else about.

I struggled to my knees, ready to get up and go to her until Lee, with one small shove of his foot, pinned me to the ground again.

'Anything?' he asked Chris.

'Same goddamn tale as our other guest,' she said and hopped off the table.

They turned to look at me. 'Hell of an escape artist, aren't you?' Chris asked.

I shrugged and said, stupidly in the circumstances, 'What have you done to her?'

'Well, what the hell does it look like?' Lee snapped and poked me with his foot again. 'Anything there to change your mind?' he asked and he strode over to Sarah who whimpered. She was absolutely terrified.

The boys crouched behind me. Darren had started to whimper too. My heart pounded in my chest and for the first time I felt more than just fear for myself. I wanted this to stop. I wanted this whole wretched business finished with. And after what he'd done to Sarah I wanted to kill Lee.

Gaz, however, was busy doing something completely different. He'd fallen with his back to me and I could feel sweaty, nervously soft hands grappling with the wire that held my wrists fast. Darren started to whimper more loudly and, agitated, began to crawl away, his face in the dirt.

'What the hell do these two know?' Chris snapped at her colleague.

Lee gave Sarah a little slap across the face before he replied. 'They found the dyke by the roadside. Pity,' he said coldly.

Gaz continued to grope at my bindings.

Sarah groaned. 'Please!' she said. 'I've told you everything. I didn't take the money.' Tears flowed down her cheeks.

'Beat you to it as well, did they? And that little shit, Megan Jones. Jesus, who can you trust? Lawyers, the same the whole goddamn world over. And where are they going, huh?' Chris growled.

Taking his cue, Lee smacked Sarah right in the face. Her head bounced back against the tyre. Blood and tears flew. I ground my teeth and experienced a sensation of hatred so strong it took my breath away. I started to make uncontrollable animal noises in my throat as I urged Gaz on. Lee looked around and laughed.

And the wire simply got tighter.

Darren, I suspected, was putting on a little show of his own. I didn't know how real his act was but the whimpers and moans and his fast face-down shuffle across the garage floor were convincing.

'But where are they going?' Chris persisted sullenly. She glanced at Darren, seemed unconcerned, and bent once more towards her captive. 'Are they taking it abroad, now, before we planned? Or are they hiding it somewhere else? Were you going to meet up with them later? After saying your little goodbyes to our friend here? I don't believe you, y'know. When did you decide to ditch me, huh?'

Sarah began to retch. Dry heaves that were more frightening than her tears. What sort of damage had they done to her?

'Oh, fetch the other one,' Chris snapped. Lee handed her his gun and strode towards the office. There was a scuffle, the sound of an angry voice and a fist connecting to flesh.

202

Silence ensued.

A moment later Lee dragged the hog-tied and protesting figure of Janice into the room.

'What the fuck are you going to do, you bastard?' I growled. 'Kidnap the whole of Calderton?'

Lee laughed. He really did have a great sense of humour. 'Would it do any good?' he asked. 'We got those photos, you know. All that scanning she was so busy with. Got ourselves the reporter too. Shame you won't see your story published.'

Janice bristled and shoved Lee with her hip. 'Fuck you,' she yelled. 'And fuck you too,' she screamed at Chris.

Lee kicked at the back of her legs and she went down on her knees, sobbing.

'Oh, for God's sake, leave her alone,' I cried. 'Haven't you done enough?'

Darren continued to crawl around the room. He was on his back now, like an upturned turtle. His hysterical groans got louder, more aggravating.

'Do something with that boy,' Chris snarled.

Lee was way overstretched. He stepped over Janice and made for the crawling Darren. Suddenly, my hands were free.

Lee reached Darren and he drew back his foot, aiming for the boy's head.

'No!' I yelled but before Lee could connect Darren flopped over sideways and dropped into the garage pit.

Lee, balance lost, tripped after him, his head slamming loudly and nauseatingly against the stone steps.

Silence from the pit.

Chris had the gun up and jammed shakily into Sarah's pale and bleeding face. 'Stop this, Lee,' she shouted. 'Lee!' The pit remained silent, not even a shuffle or a moan. 'Damnit, I've had enough.' Her voice shook along with her hand. 'You've got three seconds. Isn't that the way it goes? I count to three and you tell me where the money is, or you die. I think I've got that right, haven't I. So which is it?'

She began to count.

Chapter 30

I was too far away from Chris to do any good. She could have shot Sarah and Janice and still have time to turn the gun on me before I could get halfway across the floor. I wasn't exactly in peak physical and mental condition either.

'All right,' Sarah said through her mangled lips. Lips I'd been kissing not so very long ago. My heart groaned for her. 'Stop,' she muttered before I had to make any kamikaze decisions. She suddenly retched again. 'I'll tell you. But first, please, get me a drink. I can hardly talk.' Her tongue caught the back of her throat.

Chris looked over at the garage pit. No help there. She glanced at me. My arms were still behind my back and I looked helpless enough, I guessed; her last glance was at a malevolent but still sprawled Janice.

She waved the gun in threatening but vague circles. The weapon had looked more dangerous, more vital, somehow, in Lee's big hands.

Incredibly, Chris backed away and disappeared from sight into the office. I heard water run. Perhaps there was still a little of the Christian left in her after all.

I staggered to my feet. A second to decide and I went

to Sarah. Gaz, having managed to free his own hands, went to his friend, concealed and probably injured in the pit. Sarah shook her head vigorously as I stumbled across the floor.

'Get her,' she whispered. 'Please stop her. For me.'

I swerved past Sarah and clueless, with no plan whatsoever, barged into the office.

It's amazing what blind luck can do, isn't it? Chris was directly behind the door, trying to juggle a glass of water, a gun she wasn't confident with, and a door whose hinges hadn't been lubricated since the Gulf War. Gun and water went crashing to the ground as the door, after sticking for a moment, hit the Texan full in the face.

She swayed backwards and stumbled, heels catching the uneven wooden floorboards. The corner of the sink was perfectly aligned with her kidneys and as the metal connected with barely protected organs, I took a whole lot of pleasure in her cry of pain. She dropped to her knees, both hands going instinctively to her back.

What followed was something I would never be proud of and would never normally advocate. But these, as they say, were exceptional circumstances. My shin met her jaw in a display of hatred I hope I never experience again. But for that one moment when her head slammed sideways into the wood of the sink unit, that pleasure, that powerful feeling of vengeance filled my soul. It took every ounce of my mettle not to pound her half-conscious form into the ground.

I scrabbled around the floor looking for the gun, found it under the single bed and, not wanting to shoot myself in the foot, unlocked the back door and tossed it out into the fresh night air. Equilibrium returned a little as the weapon landed with a crash in the shrubbery beyond.

I stumbled back across the office. Chris had dragged

herself to her knees and was inching towards the back door. The fight had gone out of her, escape seemed to be all that mattered to her now.

I let her go.

I struggled back into the main room. My bandaged arm was hurting a lot by now and my neck was horribly sore after Lee's attack. My shin throbbed painfully.

Thick plumes of smoke billowed into the air. I choked on the oily smell and couldn't see a thing. The room was plunged in pitch darkness, just a steady red glow from the garage pit.

Darren!

I pulled my top up around my mouth to keep out the worst of the smoke and plunged blindly towards an intensifying mass of flame. A pair of arms suddenly encircled my legs and I let out a shriek.

'Letty,' Darren gasped. 'Come on, let's go.'

'But Gaz . . .'

'He's outside.'

'Sarah, Janice?'

'Same.'

'Lee, then. And Christine?'

'Who cares! Come on!' He caught my arm and dragged me to the front door. Flames, fuelled by spilled oil, began to lick across the concrete floor. The air got heavier, more difficult to breathe. Coughing and choking we staggered to the front door and fell through it, clutching each other.

Chapter 31

All the technology the world had to offer and we didn't have a phone between us. I never knew who rang the fire service. Flames had devoured what they could by the time the fire engines turned up.

We were all huddled together. Well, I say *all*.

Two of our number were missing.

Chris was God knows where, probably staggering around the fields of Caldervale. And Lee? At that point I didn't care.

Darren had inadvertently started the fire in the pit – some story about lighting a match to see if Lee had a pulse – he didn't, he was dead before the flames caught hold – and dropping it onto spilled fuel. But Darren had struggled out, arms still wired together. The two boys had managed to free Sarah and push her towards the door.

She'd been waiting for me when I finally got outside.

Her face was a mess. Cuts, bruises, blood everywhere. An unlovely red, yellow and green canvas.

I dragged her away from the burning building, though the flames were beginning to die down. There was probably a ton of asbestos holding it together, but

I didn't want to ponder on that unpleasant idea. The here and now was bad enough. I guided her downwards, onto an ancient tractor tyre, mildewed and almost swamped with greenery, but an improvement on the rock-hard ground.

Dwindling flames lit up her exhausted face.

I kneeled in front of her, ineffectually wiping her face with my sleeve. She was crying, great wet tears of relief and pain.

'Sarah. Oh, Sarah. How did you get involved?' I whispered.

'It wasn't supposed to happen like this.' She choked and covered her battered face with her hands. 'We were supposed to *share* the money. There was plenty for everyone. Nothing needed to change. And then Janice...' She sobbed, her words coming in short gasps. 'And you. The boys in the garage. And the photos...' She hitched a breath. 'We had to move quickly, Lorna said... word would get out. Amy... she was already suspicious... she'd been following me. Oh God,' she said and clutched at my arm. 'We found out she was a cop. I'd end up... back in prison. I couldn't stand that.'

I tried to get the gist of what she was saying. Amy's role was suddenly clear. 'Chris thought you were trying to fiddle her out of her money,' I explained. 'That's why she came after you. And me. She thought I knew.'

'We didn't get a chance to tell her, that's all.' Sarah looked up at me, begging me to understand, maybe forgive a little. She wrapped her arms across her body.

'It's all true, then?' I asked.

She nodded, swiped her arm across her nose and grimaced at the blood.

'So where is it now?'

'Safe,' she said tiredly. 'I'm going to meet Lorna later,

pick up Megan en route. I was going to make sure Chris got her share. I really was. But we have to get out now.'

'You *were* going to meet . . .' I began.

'I am. Letty, you're not going to stop me, are you?'

I glanced away from that intense and bruised face. 'I should,' I said. 'After what Lorna did to those bank workers. I don't know how you can have anything to do with her. Not after that. Not for any amount of money.'

'Letty,' she said urgently. 'That wasn't her doing, for God's sake! Why do you think everything went so wrong? Lorna was just after money. There was never any intention to harm anybody.'

I wanted to believe her. Needed to believe her, but I wasn't quite there just yet.

Sarah pushed herself off the tyre and cocked her head to one side, listening for sirens, pursuit, whatever.

'I'm not going back inside. Letty, you're going to have to knock me down to stop me leaving. Is that what you want to do? I can't defend myself.' She laughed quietly, her voice catching again. 'Usually I can, but not like this.' She turned her hands over. They were as cut and as bruised as her face.

'But why did you use me?' I asked, stomach churning. 'Is Lorna still your lover? And why has she got it in for my mum? She's made her life a fucking misery – ringing up, threatening her. She nearly got me killed on the motorway, too, thinking my mum was driving . . .'

Sarah looked up, shocked. 'Whoa, just a minute. She was never really my lover, for a kick-off. Letty, you've never been locked up. Cooped up for months on end. If you didn't have *somebody*, you'd go round the twist. We protected each other, entertained each other, the rest of the wing as well, actually. We used to put on shows. Circus act stuff. Comedy skits. She liked a laugh.' Sarah smiled to herself. 'And I never used you. You know that. There was something there for us, Letty. Surely you felt it too?'

I looked away from her bewildered face. There was a long, long pause before she went on.

'But I can't understand why you blame Lorna for your crash. After she got done for the bank job, she cut herself off from her family. If her dad wanted nothing to do with her, well, she felt exactly the same way. Trust me, she hasn't been ringing *anybody*!' She paused to take a breath and looked beyond me toward the undergrowth.

I examined her face and began to believe she was telling me the truth. 'You need to look somewhere else to solve that mystery.'

'Yes, and I know where to look,' a voice said deep from the undergrowth around the garage.

I jumped, startled, every bruised and aching muscle kicking into action.

A figure stepped into the flickering light. Lorna.

'We haven't got time for this,' Lorna said quietly. She watched my mouth as she spoke, in the same way she'd done at Sylvia's shop. She was reading my lips, I realised now. 'But if you're worried about me, Letty, you needn't be.'

I stared. I had no idea how to react.

'You need to look close to the family. My family.'

I shook my head, confused.

'I haven't got time for all this,' she repeated forcefully. 'Sarah, are you okay?' She turned to her.

Sarah's hands moved swiftly in the half light, fingers spelling letters, hands indicating words. 'A bit knocked about, nothing I can't handle,' she said aloud, for my sake, I thought. She smiled, first at Lorna and then at me.

'What do you mean? Your family?'

'I'm going to make a deal with you, Letty,' Lorna said and stepped nearer. Her hair was stuffed under a baseball cap and she wore nondescript jeans and black jacket. Her face had healed though the shadow of a bruise was just under her right eye.

'Go on,' I said.

'Let us be, please.'

'And?'

'And I'll tell you exactly who is threatening your mother. It's easy to handle, once you know that,' she said. Her voice was reasoning, convincing.

I didn't have to consider for long. I nodded. 'Who, then?'

'Remember Harry's first wife? Mary. She won't let him go. Not without a fight.' Lorna handed me a piece of paper. 'That's her address. Her business address. Her *haulage* address. She sent the lorries to scare your mum. I don't think she meant to cause such a terrible accident. I was close to her, all this jealousy has made her crazy. She needs help as much as anything,' she said sadly. 'But that's down to you.'

I nodded slowly. I'd pass the information on to Mum and the Colonel. They could handle it however they thought best.

Lorna turned to Sarah. 'Two minutes, Sarah. No longer, okay?' And with that she turned on her heels and headed back into the undergrowth.

We were silent together, staring into space. I caught worried looks from my two teenage companions and a reporter, for once at a loss, huddled nearby.

Sarah looked at me. She was clearly weighing something up. Finally, in a husky voice, she spoke out. 'Come with us, come with me.'

'Don't, Sarah...'

She reached up and touched my hair, her thumb stroked my face. I pulled her to me, gently. I couldn't resist her touch. And I had a feeling I'd never be near her again. 'Come with me,' she urged again, whispering into my ear. I felt her tears against my face. 'We're not going to get caught for this. Trust me. No one should have known about any of this. I was going to make my home here.' She hugged me to her and I stroked her back, her hair, the softness of her neck. I wanted all of her, but I didn't want the baggage that came with it.

'Think about it, Letty.' Her voice was stronger, more urgent. 'If not now, then later. Have you any idea how much money there is. You'd never have to...'

I held her tighter for a second before pushing her away, crushing that small tempted part of my soul.

'Go, if you're going,' I said in a tiny voice.

'I'll call you,' she whispered.

'Don't,' I said, tears rising in my throat.

And suddenly she turned from me. She headed towards the road, first at a trot and then at a staggering run. In seconds she was gone from sight.

Chapter 32

Amy, the lovely Amy, had been trying to stare me out for what seemed like the last ten minutes. I managed to hold her gaze by concentrating on the furrow between her eyes.

'Smoke?' she asked.

'It's a government building,' I pointed out. 'I didn't think it was allowed.'

She sighed and sat back in the comfortless wooden chair of the interview room. The fresh preppy clothes had been replaced by an austere suit, clinically white shirt and a face free of makeup. She looked so different that at first I thought it wasn't the same woman.

I'd been in this room before. When Emma Auckland had taken a statement about the motorway crash, so the place wasn't as scary as it might have been.

The police surgeon – the same surgeon who'd opined that Lee was dead before the flames got to him, though the coroner would have to confirm it – had given me a quick once-over and pronounced me battered but fit for questioning.

Amy manoeuvred the tape machine into the centre of the table. Her companion, a DCI from Halifax, tried not to look bored. Emma stood at the head of the room,

214

guarding the door in case the SAS decided to rescue me.

We'd already been round in circles a few times.

I'd been cautioned, as had my three companions. Gaz's mother had been summoned from the BT call centre where she worked and Vince had turned up to either support or wallop Darren, I wasn't sure which. Janice's editor had arrived, as had a worried AnnaMaria. She'd been driving round Calderton with a bewildered Julia, looking for me. So it was quite a diverse group that awaited our release from the Calderton cop shop.

'So you don't know where the money might be?' Amy, Baptist lay preacher and police undercover specialist demanded.

'It's in some blankets, somewhere between here and I don't know where. In a Mercedes van, maybe two, with Aid Convoy written all over them. So it shouldn't be that hard to find. Even for you.' I overcame my painfully croaking voice and smiled sweetly at the policewoman.

She ignored my snide comment. 'Why do you think it's in that particular van?'

I paused, ready with a lie. I didn't want to drop Darren and Gaz into it any more than necessary so I repeated my story of the previous afternoon spent at Tyre and Tread, reminding her of the type of van Liz/Lorna had been working on. I didn't bother telling her that the boys had seen the van being loaded up before they helped themselves to some of the loot. I'd deny I knew that until I was blue in the face.

Fortunately, me, Janice and the boys had had plenty of time to cook up a story. A story that hovered around the truth but didn't involve my companions in any negative sense. They'd saved my life – not once, but twice – and if they were to make a small financial gain, well, that was okay with me.

Janice with a headstart on all the other media that had descended on Calderton had a cracking story, one that linked up nicely with the Calderton Aid Convoy spread and CFC Health and Beauty.

I had to tell the truth about Sarah Flowers and some of what I knew about Lorna. I couldn't help Amy much with Megan but I was happy to tell her about Chris F Crozier and Lee, her vicious, violent and quite dead colleague.

Christine's father had received an unexpected international phone call and apparently he was on the next flight over. I had a feeling he'd pass his daughter at thirty thousand feet going in the opposite direction. Rumour had it that the CFC manager's post was up for grabs and Sue, Megan's secretary, had got her CV printed and ready. She'd probably get the job too.

'Do you want your solicitor?' Amy asked, after my explanations.

I laughed. 'The missing Megan Jones, you mean?'

'The duty solicitor,' Amy said coldly.

I leaned across the desk. 'As long as they're not as homophobic as you.' I sneered as best I could. As yet, neither of us had warmed to the other. It was unlikely we ever would.

I got a solicitor – supplied by Julia – and signed a statement, a copy of which I carefully stashed in my jeans. I was then released, still under caution. So far, I was under suspicion of breaking and entering, obstructing a police inquiry, withholding evidence and, if Amy got her way, being a lesbian. But with Julia's brief on the case I felt I was in the winning corner. I didn't want to dwell on the possibility that I too might see the inside of Styal prison.

But as investigations were ongoing, we would have to wait and see.

Chapter 33

Everyone – except Amy – still hoping for closure on the whole business, got an invite to Mrs Buckham's grand shop reopening, including my smartly turned-out heroes, Gaz and Darren. The transformation of both the shop and the boys was complete.

'I got the idea from a book, you know,' Sylvia informed me as she bustled about stocking new pine shelves with 'English Heritage' produce and filling barrels with home-produced spuds, dutifully rolled in soil for that authentic 'organic' look. Even the tinned beans she was piling high were organically grown. The cheese was local, the veg phosphorous free and the floor groaned under the weight of all those groceries. I couldn't resist a quick check of the polished pine floorboards. No clues as to any wrongdoing left at all, although it was now obvious where the bank loot had been stashed.

The eggs Mrs Buckham had bought from me had had similar treatment to the King Edwards. I usually removed all the hen shit and sticky feathers before selling the free-rangers on, but this time the process was reversed.

The muckier the better, Mrs Buckham reckoned. Farm produced eggs looked more authentic if they could be seen to have come straight from a chicken's backside.

Mrs Buckham interrupted my reverie as she elbowed her way through the crowd. 'Well, I never did understand why my floorboards were still up,' she said. I'd explained the whole palaver to her, though I think some of the finer points went over her head. 'Should never have trusted Frankie Field. There's only him could come up with the idea of hiring an escaped prisoner to do a bit of woodwork.'

As I said, she'd missed some of the finer points. 'And that Amy,' she whispered. 'Only met her those couple of times. Never liked her, never liked her face. Should have known she was a cop. She's the type that could cause trouble in an empty house.'

Sylvia buttoned her lip for a moment as a villager edged past, heading for the cheese sandwiches.

'And what about your Sarah, eh? Bit of a dark horse that one. Are you likely to see her again?' she asked, not so innocently.

'Oh, I doubt it,' I said and once again I felt a sharp twinge of regret.

Despite its refit, the shop had retained a few original features, including a window full of local adverts. In the midst of her grand opening, the proprietor herself clutched a small square of card, neatly printed in felt-tip and ready to join the display in the window.

'Not sure about this one,' Sylvia said.

I took a swallow of the organic wine she'd provided for the opening and grimaced at the overpoweringly bitter gooseberry flavour. Somehow I think she'd confused 'organic' with 'home-made'. Not the same thing at all.

'What do you think?' she asked.
I read the note.

OLD T-SHIRTS WANTED:
FERRETS FIRST!
HOME FOR RESCUE FERRETS
Little Lane Farm, Langton
MAKES IDEAL BEDDING
CALL 224 5611 OR SEE PROP

I thought for a minute of Anne, but she was in London, having moved at last.

'Looks all right. What's the problem?' I enquired as my lips, drawn back into a rictus by the wine, began to regain their normal shape.

'More use in an orphanage, if you ask me. Now there's something that should have gone to Eastern Europe,' she said, a twinkle in her eye. 'Not that I begrudge a ferret a T-shirt –'

The phone interrupted her and I volunteered to answer it. It was that or laugh in her face.

Thoughtlessly I took another swig of wine, so my 'Good afternoon, Calderton Corner Shop,' was a bit strangled, though that didn't stop my voice from being recognised.

'Letty?' the caller whispered. 'It's Sarah.'

Established in 1978, The Women's Press publishes
high-quality fiction and non-fiction from outstanding women
writers worldwide. Our list spans literary fiction, crime
thrillers, biography and autobiography, health, women's
studies, literary criticism, mind body spirit, the arts and the
Livewire Books series for young women.
Our bestselling annual *Women Artists Diary* features the best
in contemporary women's art.

The Women's Press also runs a book club through
which members can buy, every quarter, the best fiction and
non-fiction from a wide range of British publishing houses,
mostly in paperback, always at discount.

To receive our latest catalogue, or for information on
The Women's Press Book Club, send a large SAE to:

The Sales Department
The Women's Press Ltd
34 Great Sutton Street London EC1V 0LQ
Tel: 020 7251 3007 Fax: 020 7608 1938
www.the-womens-press.com

Alma Fritchley
Chicken Run
The first Letty Campbell mystery

When Letty Campbell warily agrees to let her land be used for
a classic car auction, she has no idea what lies ahead. Why is
her gorgeous ex, Julia, really so desperate for the auction to
happen? Is the new love of Julia's life as suspicious as she
seems? And why does Letty have a horrible feeling that she
should never have got involved?

'Irrepressibly bouncy' *Pink Paper*

'A breath of fresh air . . . Alma Fritchley is a talent
to watch' *Crime Time*

Crime Fiction £5.99
ISBN 0 7043 4691 5

Alma Fritchley
Chicken Feed
The second Letty Campbell mystery

When Letty's lover Anne sets off for a US-wide lecture tour,
Letty prepares for a mournful few weeks alone on the farm
with only her chickens for company. But her peace is
shattered by the arrival of a strange woman in her kitchen
with a wild and appealing five-year-old child. Before she
knows it, their troubles are hers and Letty is caught up in a
sequence of rapid, outrageous and dangerous events. Why
has charismatic lesbian politician Sita Joshi suddenly
disappeared? How come Letty's gorgeous ex-lover Julia has
wound up in jail? What has it got to do with the top lesbian
singer recently in town? And what is on the video tape that
turns up in the village and almost costs Letty her life . . . ?

'A terrific yarn . . . mightily recommended' *Diva*

'This book had me laughing out loud' *Crime Time*

Crime Fiction £5.99
ISBN 0 7043 4692 3

Alma Fritchley
Chicken Out
The third Letty Campbell mystery

When Letty's ancient neighbour, George, dies in suspicious circumstances, village tongues start to wag. Can it really be coincidence that George's glamorous niece, Stephanie, suddenly appeared just hours before George met his death? And who is the elderly Cousin Flo, who has also turned up out of the blue?

Trapped into arranging an unusual funeral and struggling against Stephanie's considerable charms, Letty wishes that she was not involved. But as a series of dramatic revelations unfold, she becomes embroiled in a dangerous case involving mysterious letters, hidden treasures – and a secret lesbian love affair . . .

'Hilarious' *Evening Standard*

Crime Fiction £6.99
ISBN 0 7043 4619 2

Marcia Muller
Listen to the Silence
A Sharon McCone mystery

Only in the aftermath of her father's death does McCone
uncover a family secret kept for forty years – that her parents
adopted her and that her true roots lie elsewhere. She has
never faced a more urgent quest than the one to trace her
birth parents. But the trail leads her deep into Native
American country – and to the heart of a feud where murder,
undisturbed for years, is now overlaid with fresh violence.

'Sharon McCone was created 20 years ago, and
remains the first and the best of the school of
tough female private eyes' *Crime Time*

Crime Fiction £6.99
ISBN 0 7043 4672 9

Val McDermid
Common Murder
The second Lindsay Gordon crime thriller

A protest group hits the headlines when unrest explodes into
murder. Already on the scene, local journalist Lindsay Gordon
desperately tries to strike a balance between personal and
professional responsibilities. As she peels back the layers of
deception surrounding the protest and its opponents, she finds
that no one – ratepayer or reporter, policeman or peace
woman – seems wholly above suspicion. Then Lindsay
uncovers a truth that even she can scarcely believe . . .

'Pacey and wittily written . . . bound to make
McDermid one of Britain's favourite detective
writers' *Options*

'Val McDermid is an inspiration' *Herald*

Crime Fiction £5.99
ISBN 0 7043 4592 7

Val McDermid
Booked for Murder
The fifth Lindsay Gordon crime thriller

The freak 'accident' that killed bestselling author Penny
Varnavides takes on a more sinister aspect when police
discover that her latest unpublished novel featured murder by
the same means. Of the handful of people who knew the plot,
the prime suspect is wise enough to call in her old friend,
journalist Lindsay Gordon, to uncover the truth that lies
behind the seething rivalries and desperate power games that
infect the publishing world . . .

'Has the reader gripped from the first page . . .
both moody and hilarious and thoroughly
unpredictable' *Tribune*

'The writing is tough and colourful, the scene
setting excellent' *Times Literary Supplement*

Crime Fiction £5.99
ISBN 0 7043 4595 1

Manda Scott
Hen's Teeth
A Kellen Stewart crime thriller

Shortlisted for the Orange Prize for Fiction and the First Blood Award

Midnight in Glasgow. A bad time to be faced with a dead body. Especially if the body in question is your ex-lover and the woman grieving at her bedside used to be your friend. Add a corpse packed with Temazepam, a genetic engineer with a strange interest in chickens and a killer on the loose with a knife, and you have all the reasons you need to walk away and never come back.

Except that it's Bridget who's dead and she has always deserved better than that. For Dr Kellen Stewart, ex-medic, ex-lover and ex-friend, a simple call for help rapidly twists into a tangled web of death and deceit . . .

'Eloquent, excellent . . . A new voice for a new world and it's thrilling' **Fay Weldon**

Crime Fiction £5.99
ISBN 0 7043 4685 0

Ellen Hart
Wicked Games
A Jane Lawless crime thriller

When Jane Lawless takes a new tenant into her house, she
has no idea what lies ahead. Shortly after Elliot Beauman
moves in, Jane and her friend Cordelia find themselves drawn
inexorably into the Beaumans' lives – and discover a trail of
death and destruction in their wake . . .

Wicked Games is a dark and compelling crime thriller by one
of the most acclaimed writers in the field.

'The psychological maze of a Barbara Vine mystery'
Publishers Weekly

'The mysteries pile up so relentlessly that you'll
just have to wait and see who gets caught without a
seat in the game of murderous chairs' **Kirkus Reviews**

'Her style is tight and hypnotic. Her action brisk
and riveting' **Washington Blade**

Crime Fiction £6.99
ISBN 0 7043 4590 0